P9-CNE-186
3 4028 08712 4005
HARRIS COUNTY PUBLIC LIBRARY

J Selzni
Selznick, Brian
The Marvels

WITHDRAWN

$32.99
ocn897016494
First edition.   09/28/2015

You either see it or you don't.

You either see it or you don't

This book belongs to:

_____

★ THE ★
MARVELS

BRIAN SELZNICK

★

SCHOLASTIC PRESS · NEW YORK

17

66

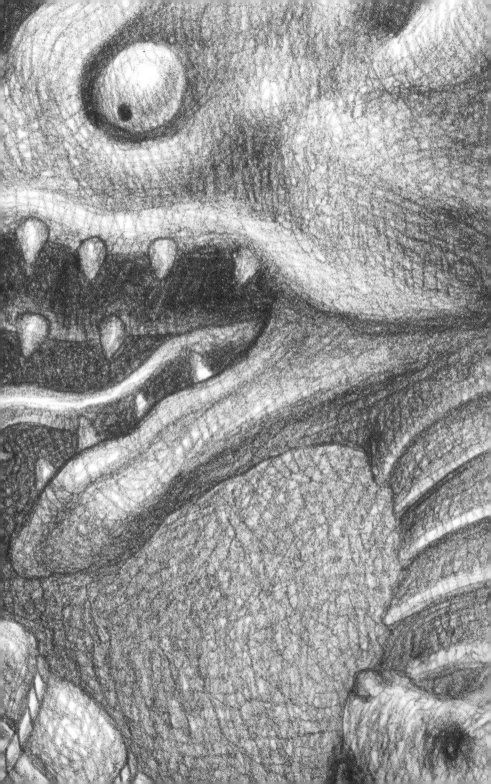

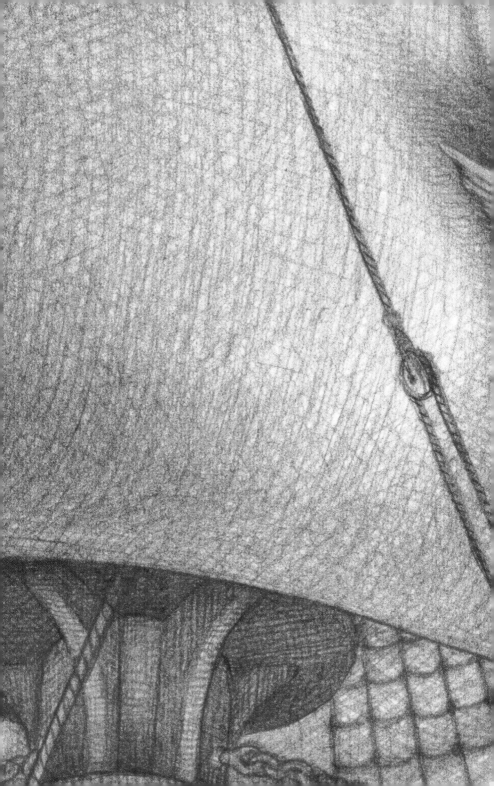

ATTENTION

One ni
on

THE

the Ang

the Ang

The

SAILORS

t only

BOARD

RAKEN

and

the *Dragon*

PLAY.

formance begins

at midnight

reenacts the battle

good and evil

until only

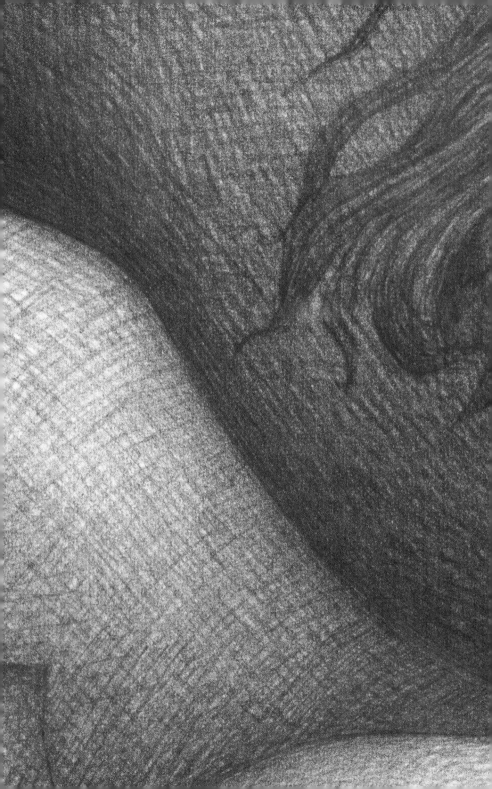

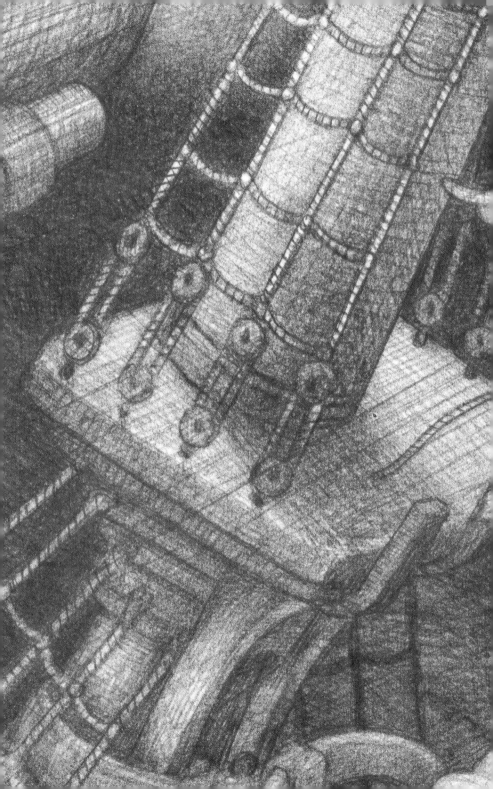

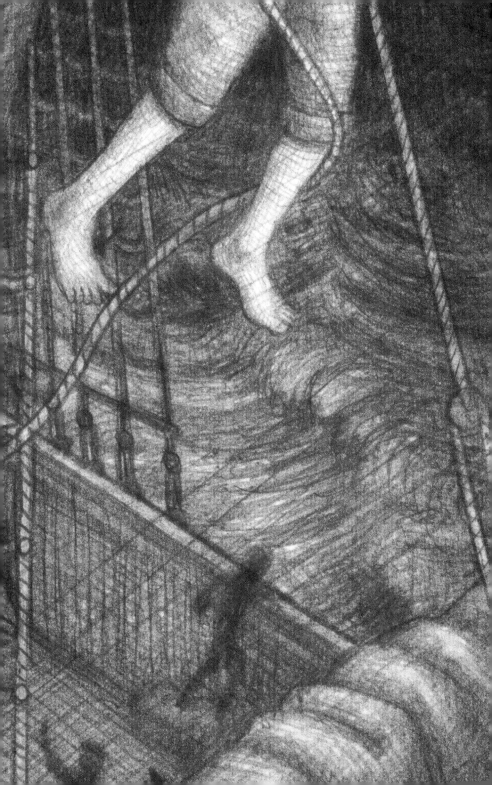

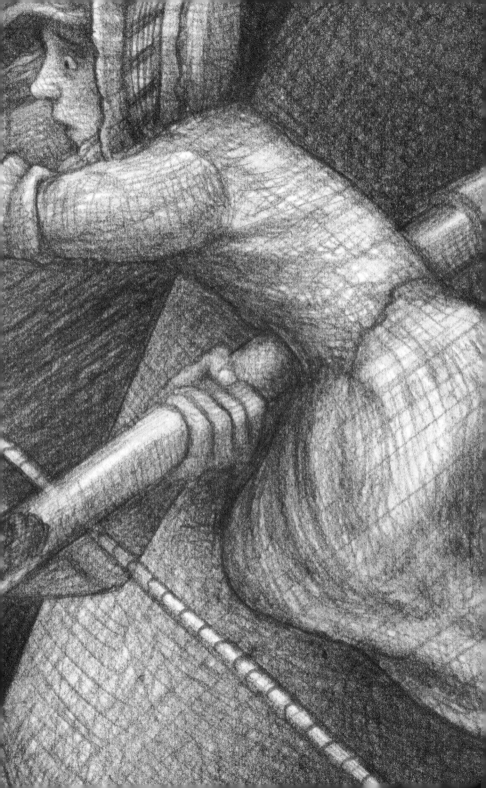

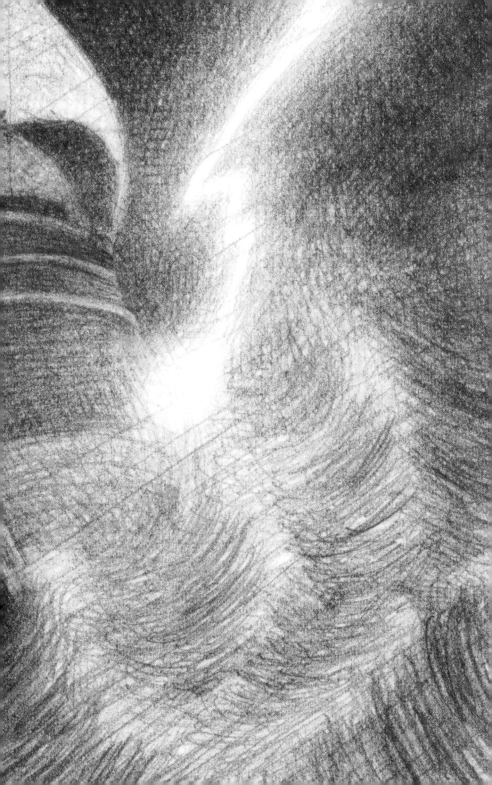

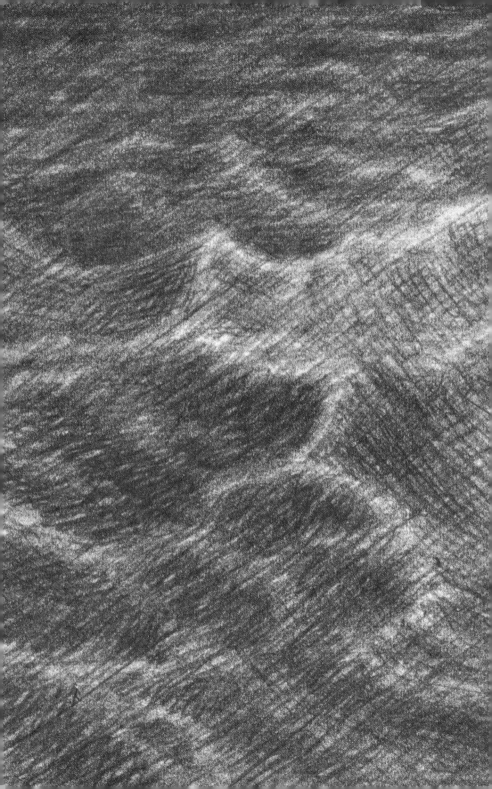

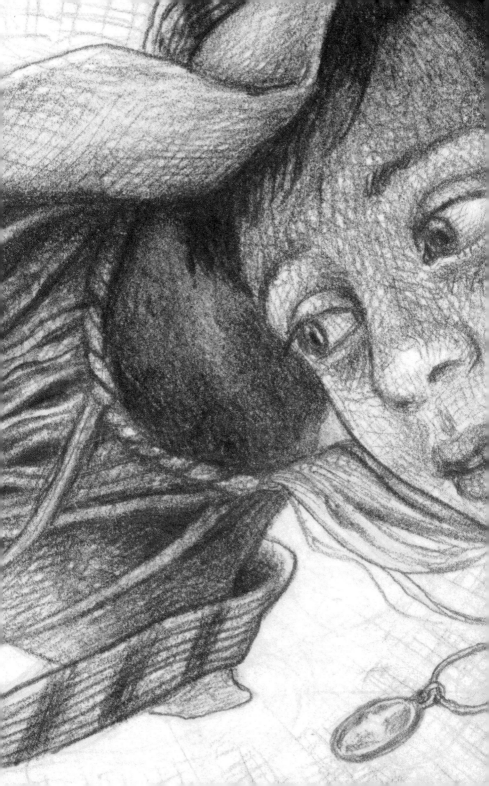

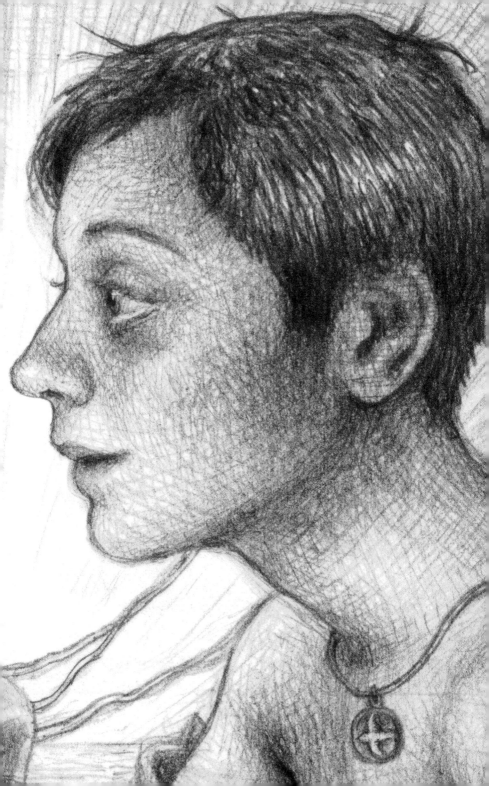

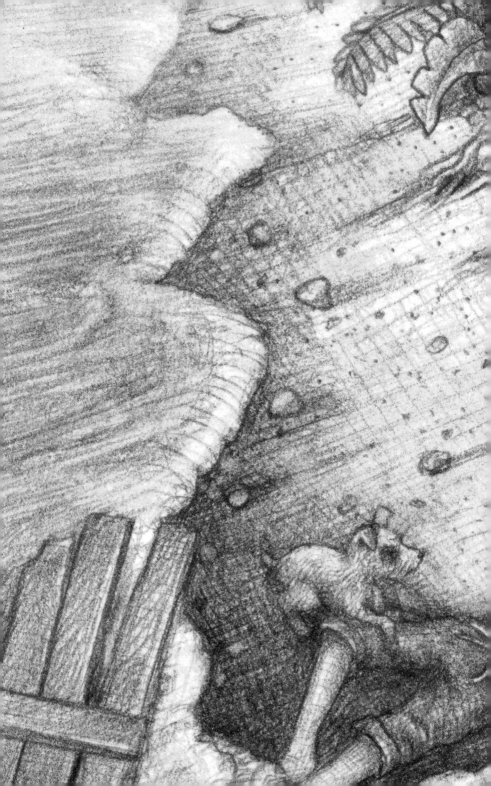

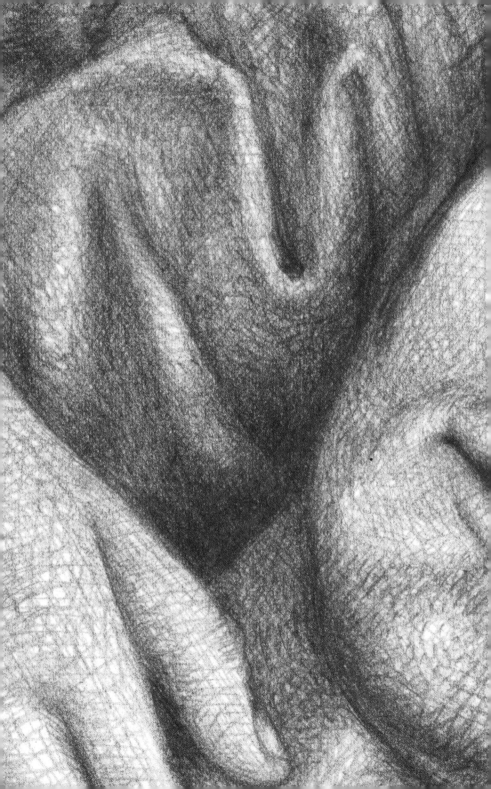

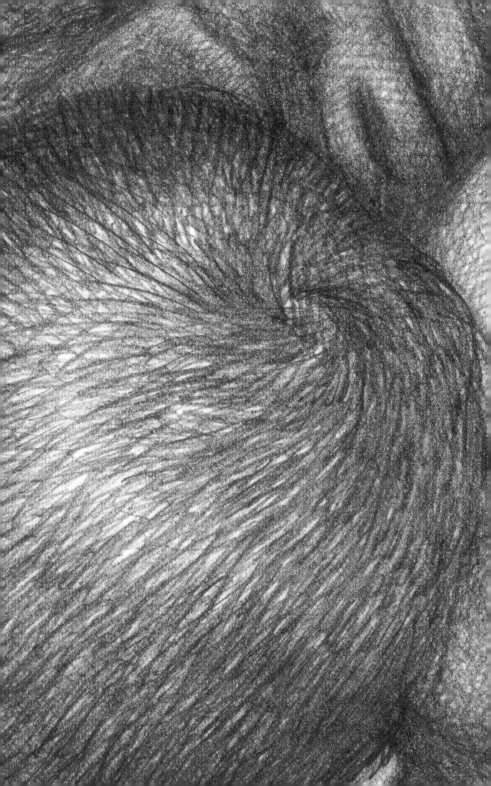

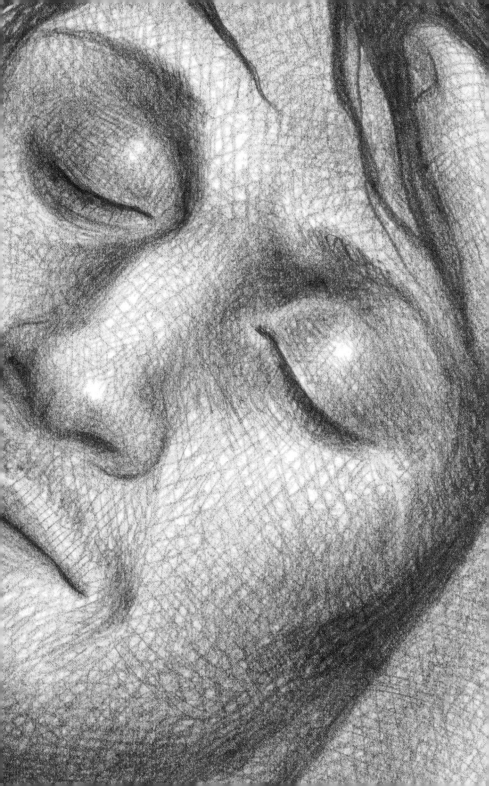

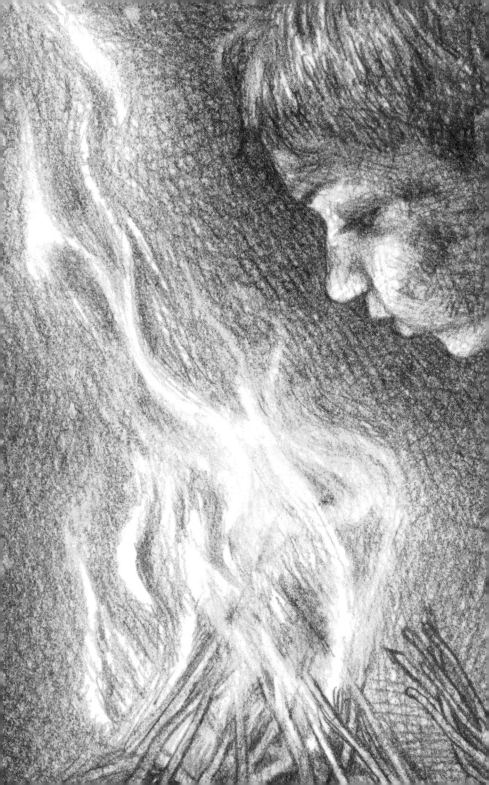

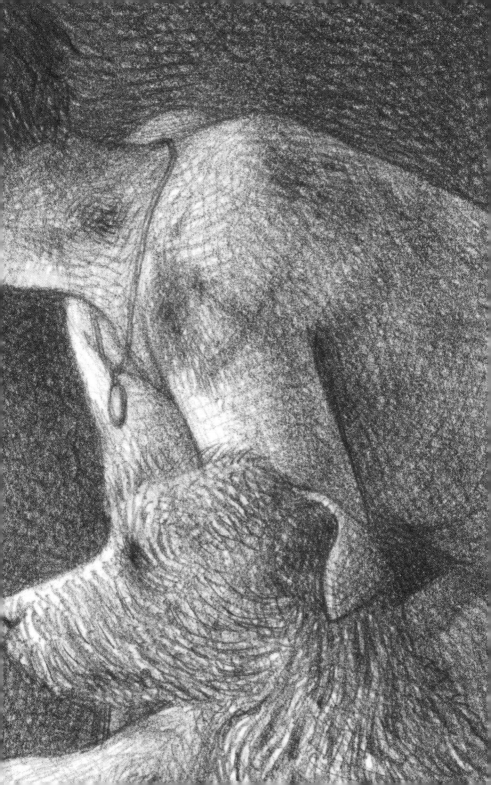

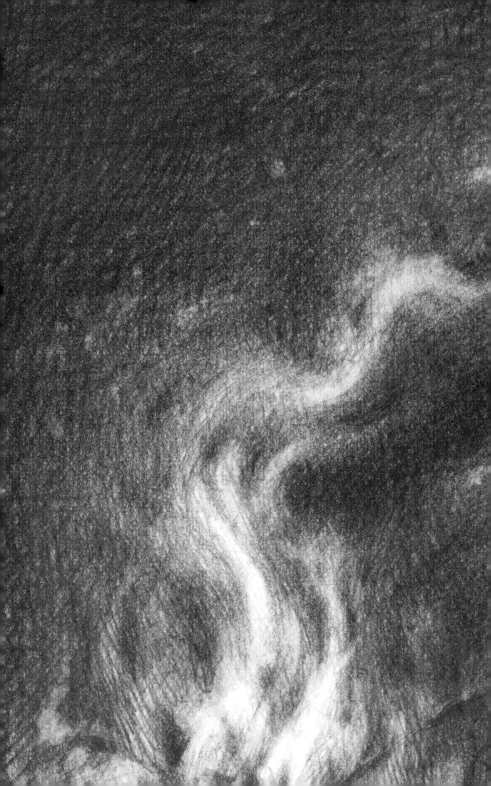

ACCOUNT OF THE GREAT LOSS

—

According to the latest reports, a twelve-year-old boy named **Billy Marvel** and his dog, **Tar**, were the only survivors of the American whaling ship the Kraken. The child, exhausted and delirious, told a wondrous tale involving angels, dragons, lightning, and thunder, most of which was surely a dream inspired by the real terror he experienced at sea. Saved by an English ship and brought to London, he gave his account through tears, shed no doubt over the loss of s... During his interview, Tar, sat faithfully by... gave his mast...

one of the lost named Marcus floated in the island, where buried in the ship to long v broth sto w

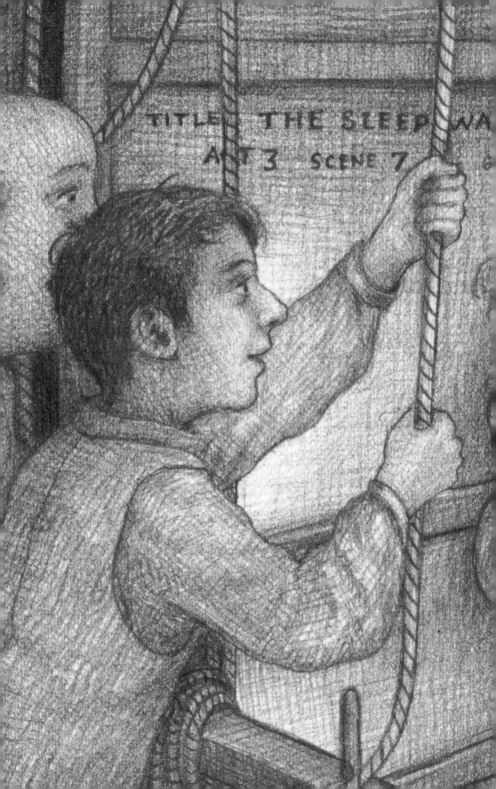

HERE LIES
TAR
A GOOD DOG
AND TRUE

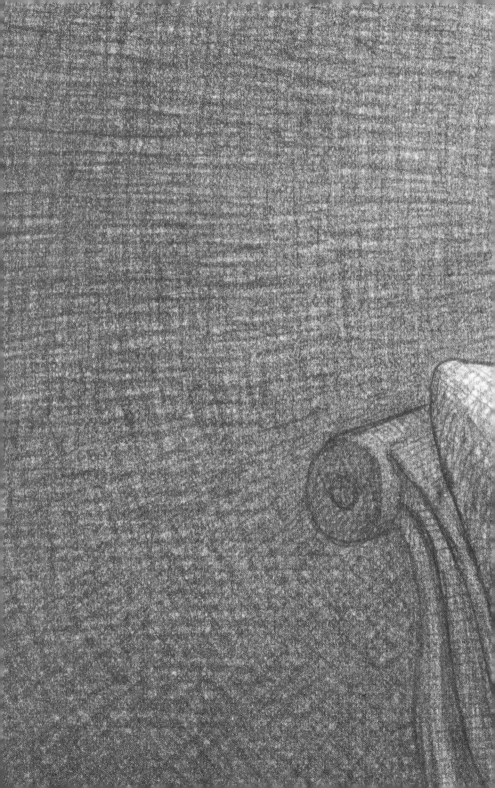

HERE LIES
TAR

A GO
AND

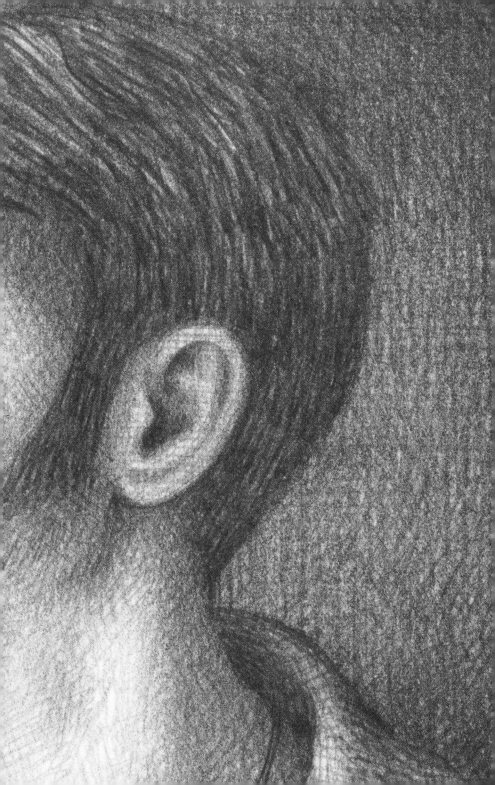

Marriage

LONDON DIOCESE }

MARRIED HERE

Groom Marcus Marvel

Son of Billy Marvel

Made the oath that he

Bride Catherine Vin

Daughter of Harold

that he k

ON THIS DATE
10th June 1800

THIS DAY

Red Eyes Blue
air
(Unknown)
d

tendeth to marry

Hair Yellow Eyes
ine and Ba

veth no lawful reason t
er the said intended marriag

ROOM

A MEMORABLE DEBUT! EXTRA

Young Mr. Alexander Marvel, only four years old, unexpectedly made his debut when he toddled out on stage naked as the day he was born while his parents, the famed actors Marcus and Catherine Marvel, were performing in their hit play The Vicar's Tea. The naked child, as red-haired as his father, surprised actors and audience alike. After slipping away from his minders, he appeared just as his father was about to give the famous speech about the withered hand. It goes without saying that the terrifying mood dissolved immediately with great gusts of rollicking laughter.

12th Sept 1812

My dear Mama

I am sorry I caught the mouse and put it in your make-up box. Papa punished me by taking away my toy theatre and he said to write this le...

1815 {

The exuberant redheade young actor Alexande Marvel stole the show las night when he accidentally li one of the harem girls on fire with his torch. No one was injured, but after the screaming subsided there was much merriment all around.

ANNIVERSARY ANTICS · 1821

THIS year marks the fifty fifth anniversary of the Royal Theatre, which celebrated with a revival of its first play, The Haunted Tower. Alexander Marvel, well known to London audiences for his rich and lively impersonations and many newsworthy antics, seemed to be having a little too much fun poking and pinching a chorus girl when he thought no one was looking. This led to an unrehearsed moment when a silk umbrella was used as a weapon and the leading lady was forced to intervene

11ᵗʰ Nov 1821

1829 *ONLY SURVIVOR*

Billy Marvel, seventy-five years of age, died last night of a stroke. Mr. Marvel was the only survivor of the famous shipwreck of the Kraken, which so captivated the world in the middle of the last century. His grandson, the troubled actor Alexander Marvel, was recently in the news aga... himself for jumping off th... stage during a performance ... A Midsummer Night's Drea... and punching the father of ... crying child. The scene th... ensued in the audience w... worthy of anything ever ... presented on stage ...

A Midsummer

STARRING
ALEXANDER
MARVEL
AS
OBERON
King of the Faeries

er **Nights**

Dream

SHOCKING RETURN

1835 · After two years in jail for the attempted murder of a stage manager, Alexander Marvel returns to the stage. Never before has an actor been so closely associated with a role as Mr. Marvel is with the faerie king Oberon in Shakespeare's play A Midsummer Night's Dream. Of course, after the untimely deaths of his parents – the

celebrated actors Marcus and Catherine Marvel, in a stagecoach accident that left the entire nation in tears – England needed a new sta Mr. Marvel first played Oberon in 1829, the ye he began what many was his descent int madness when he jumped off the s without

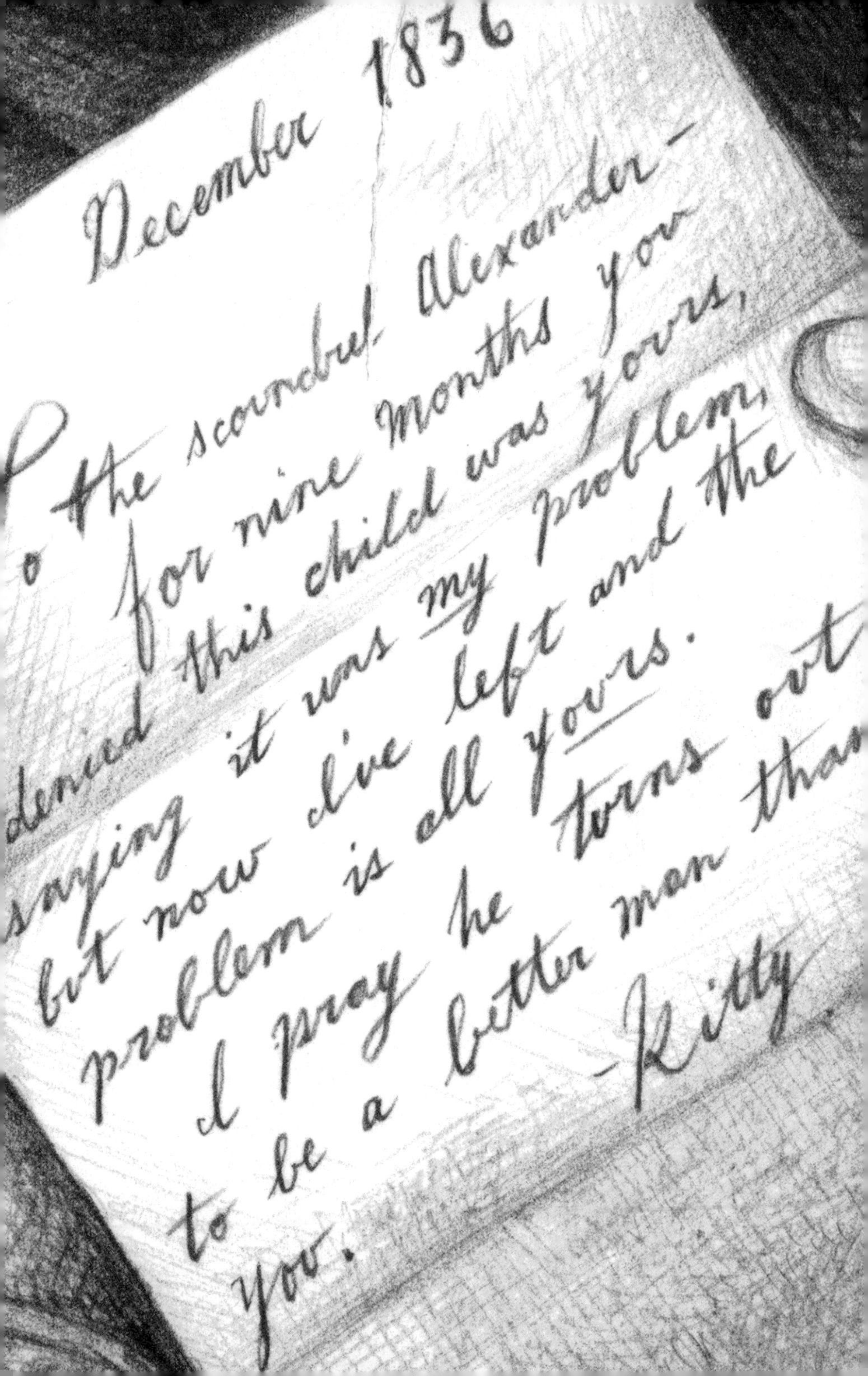

December 1836

To the scoundrel Alexander—

for nine months you
denied this child was yours,
saying it was *my* problem,
but now I've left and the
problem is all yours.
I pray he turns out
to be a better man than
you.

—Kitty

LONDON NEWS

SATURDAY 1 SEPTEMBER 1885

FOURTH GENERATION OF THEATRE DYNASTY TAKES THE STAGE

Tonight at 8:00 p.m., the great actor Oberon Marvel, himself the son of the infamous and insane actor Alexander Marvel, grandson of the beloved Marcus Marvel, and great-grandson of Billy Marvel, the sole survivor of the Kraken disaster, will reprise the role that made him a star here and abroad. He will of course be playing tragic King Leontes in The Winter's Tale by Shakespeare. The public went wild for his performance when he last played the part, creating a frenzy among theatregoers not seen in a generation, since his own father played King Oberon in A Midsummer Night's Dream, the part for which he was named.

At Oberon's side will be his great partner in love and on stage Eleanora Marvel. She will play poor Hermione, his innocent queen. Who can forget the stunning scene where the statue of the long-dead queen miraculously comes to life, reuniting her with the regretful King Leontes?

Tears still come to our eyes when we think about that moment. Not even Duse or Bernhardt have captured the imagination of the public Eleanora

LEGACY

THEATRE
TS

No. 16352 Vol. XXXIV

Oberon and Eleanora Marvel in The Winter's Ta

30 JANUARY '88

CARTE

Dearest One—
I trust you are
feeling better—
I do hate to
travel and
perform without
you—Love Oberon

Mrs Ele
18 I
Lond
E

N

1888

IS IT TRUE?
Eleanora Marvel, t
world-famous actre
is rumoured to t
pregnant.

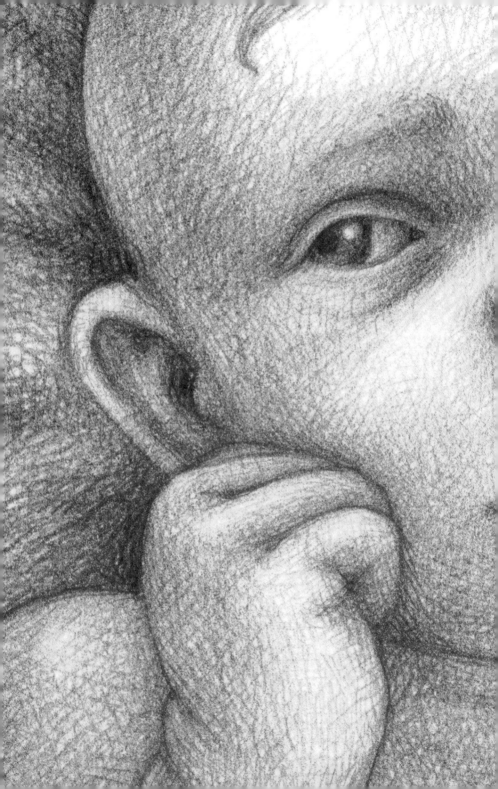

THEATRE'S KI
WELCOME

FAMOUS FAMILY'S FIFTH GENERATION

Oberon and Eleanora Marvel, the greatest performers of this or any age, announced the arrival of a son named Leontes, on 10 November. The child, red-haired like the previous generations of his family, was named for his father's greatest role, King Leontes in The Winter's Tale, the same way that Oberon before him was named for HIS father's most famous role, the faerie king Oberon in A Midsummer Night's Dream. This strange series of characters, kings, fathers, and red-headed sons leads us to wonder what name Leontes will give his own son in the future... Hamlet perhaps? Macbeth or Romeo? Only time will

Oberon and Eleano

No. 16508 Vol. XXXVII

G AND QUEEN
EW PRINCE

arvel with Leontes

tell. Of course, the real thrill will be in watching this lucky child as he grows up and discovers his great family history, the strands of time that reach from him all the way back to the unforgettable shipwreck of 1766.

GRANDFATHER MYSTERY

The child's grandfather, the notorious Alexander Marvel, disappeared from public view many years ago and his death has never been confirmed. Whispered stories circulate around the Royal Theatre, where sightings of his ghost have been reported, although many believe he is living like a hermit beneath the stage, reliving his greatest triumphs in a wild state of madness and confusion. What other mysteries are to be found in the dusty

CRYING BABY MAKES DEBUT

Last night at the Royal Theatre, a surprising sound came from backstage during the climax of its current drama: a crying baby! The sound, reported to be the new son of Oberon and Eleanora Marvel, pierced the dramatic silence as the knife Mr. Marvel held was about to be plunged into the heart of the

Child Misses His Only Cue!

ENTIRE AUDIENCE CONFUSED

In what was billed as his professional stage debut, the young Leontes Marvel, four years old, misse his only cue, leaving his parents, the celebr actors Oberon and Eleanora Marvel, scramb improvise. After several minutes of awkward during which stagehands could be seen

e,

cage

WHERE

FATHER SHAKES WITH AN?
B.

In what is becomin?
game, Leontes Marv?
again went missing
latest production of
Playing the doomed
child reduced his l?
pacing back and forth

S LEO?

BEFORE
GING DOWN CURTAIN

a national parlour
known as Leo, once
ckstage during the
he *Winter's Tale*.
oung prince, the
ndary parents to
stage whil

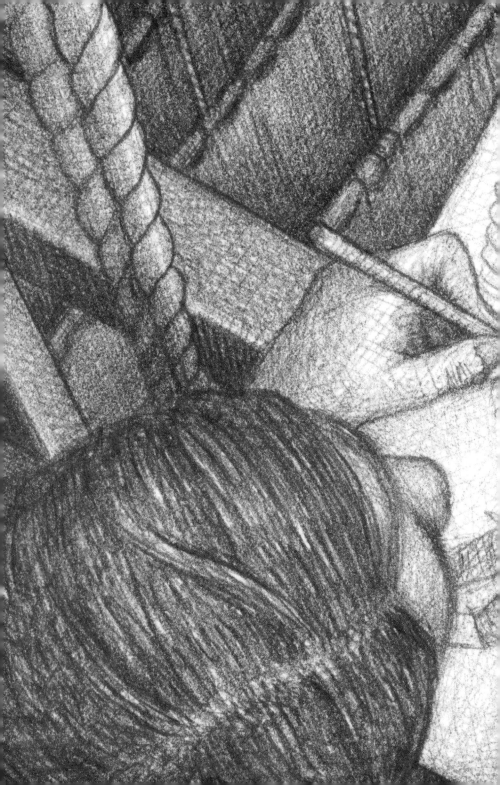

DRESSIN
ROOA

CURRENT
PRODUCTION—
THE
TEMPEST
BY WM. SHAKESPEARE
STARRING
OBERON & ELEANOR
MARVEL

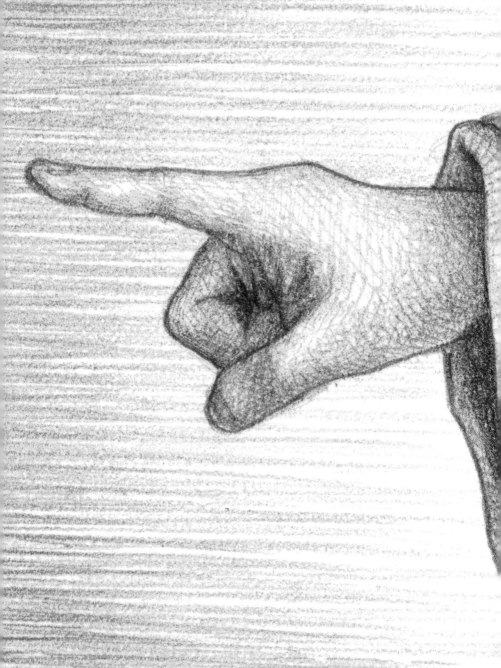

BANIS

• TheatreWo

PERFORMAN

[LATE NIG

Rumours are circulating throughout th
theatre world today that the brilliant
but bedevilled actor Oberon Marvel has
finally banished his wayward son, Leonte
from the stage forever. After years of misse
cues, forgotten lines, awkward scenes and en
barrassing moments, it seems as if the boy
father has had enough. A particularly distressin
moment in the middle of *The Tempest* wa

HED!

ld In Shock •

ES CANCELLED

REPORT]

ollowed by forty minutes of screaming
rom backstage, witnesses reported.

LEGACY IN DOUBT

Vhat will become of this child, born
into a family of flame-haired geniuses,
eemingly destined for greatness, but now
xpelled from the only world he has known?

...summer

STARRING
ALEXANDER
MARVEL
~ AS ~
OBERON
King of the Faeries

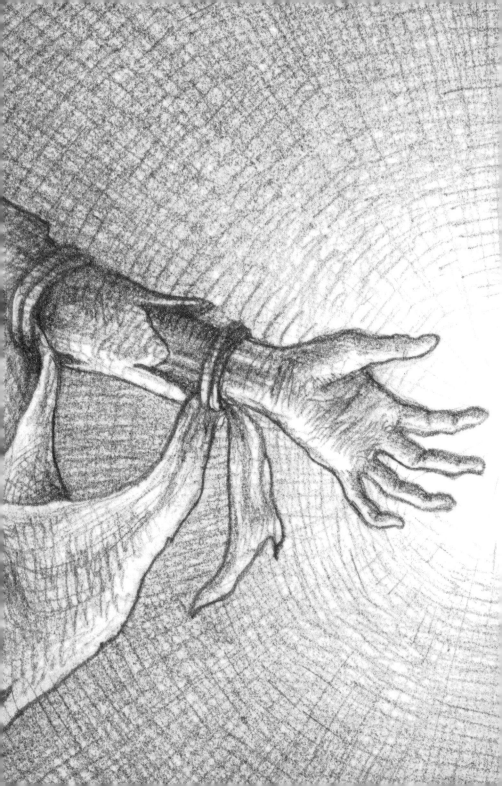

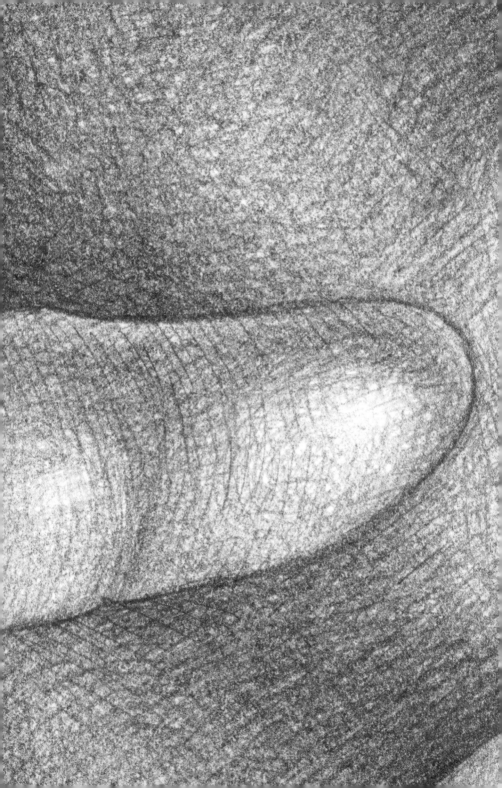

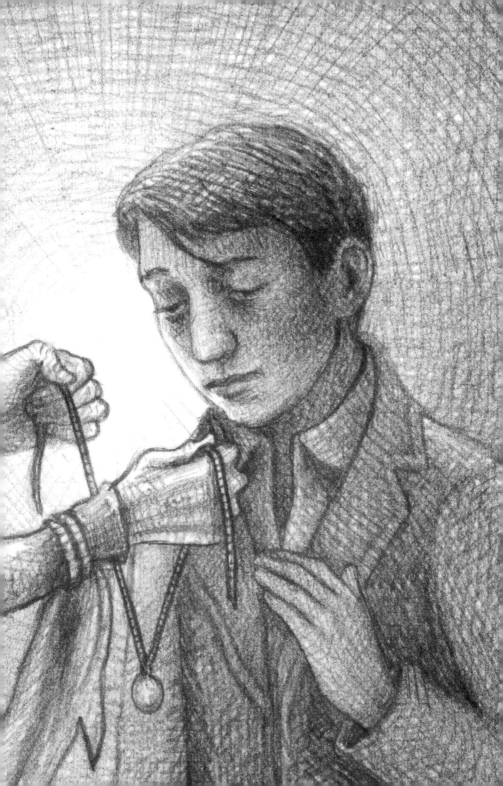

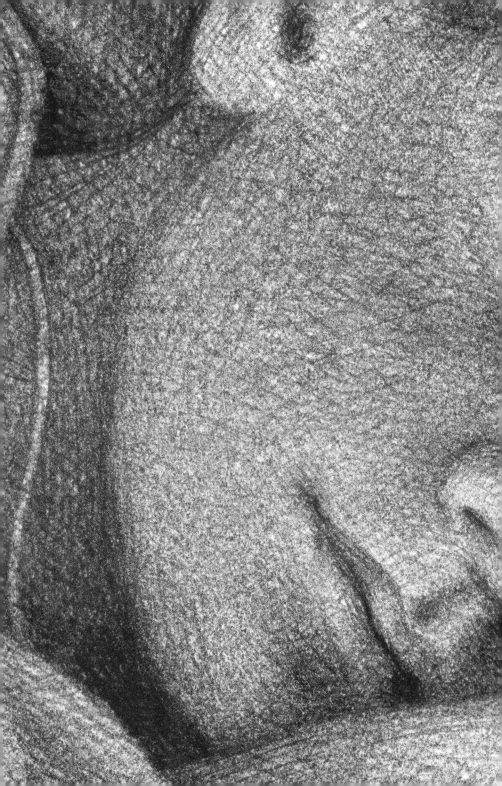

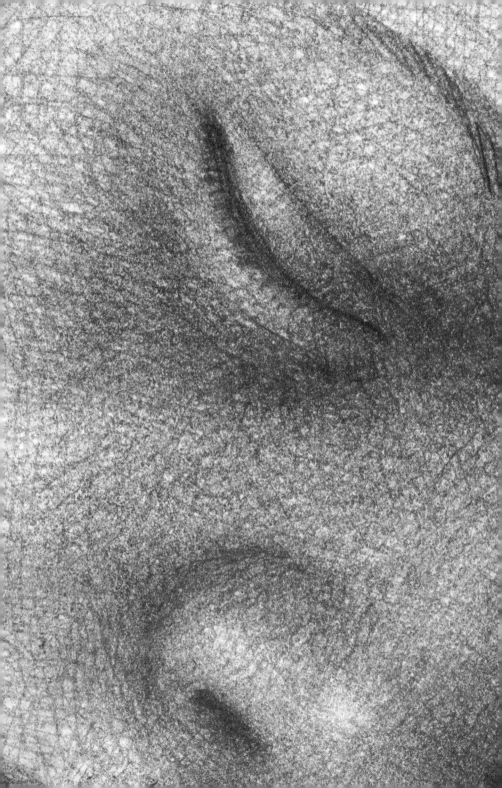

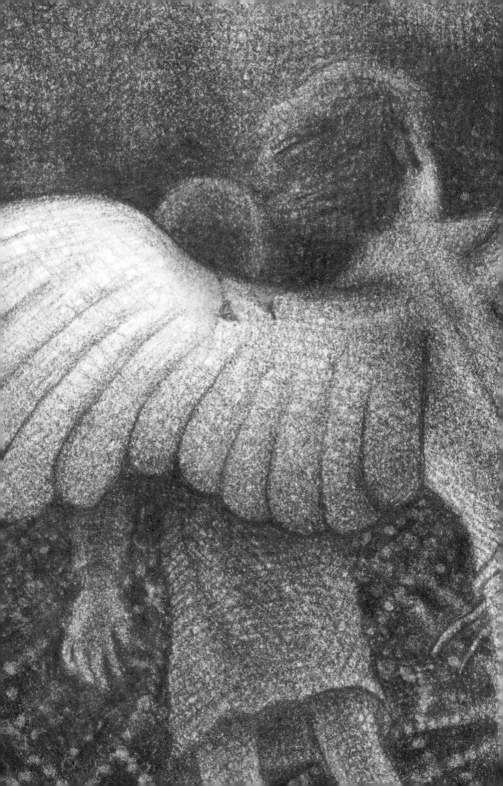

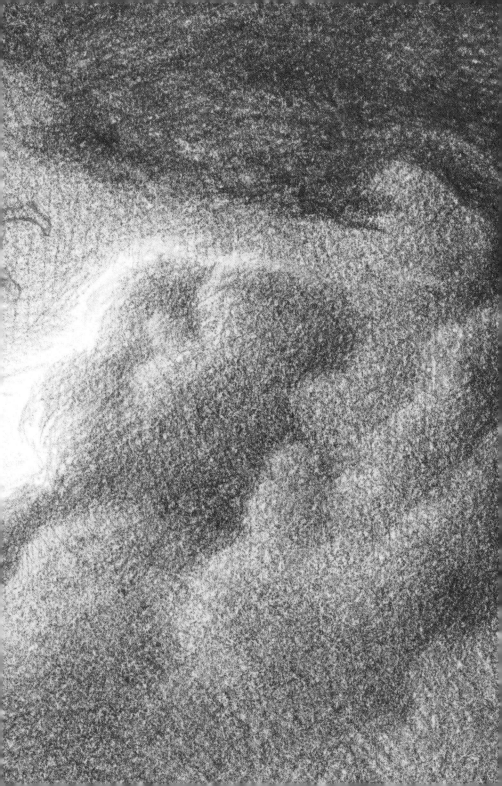

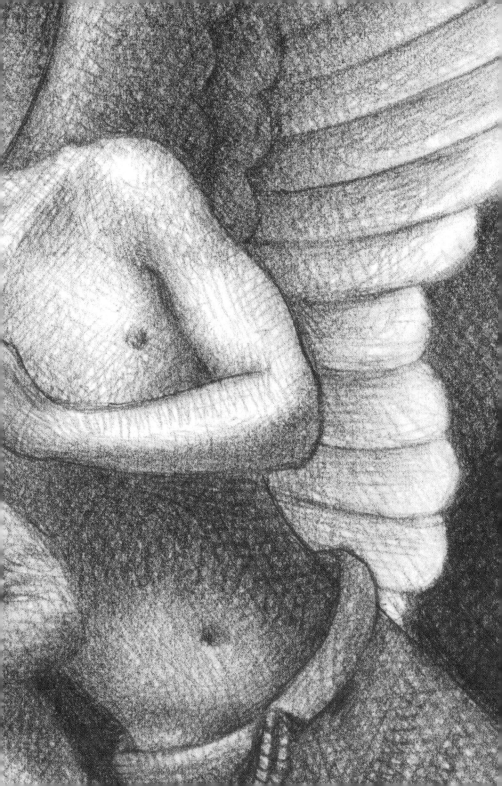

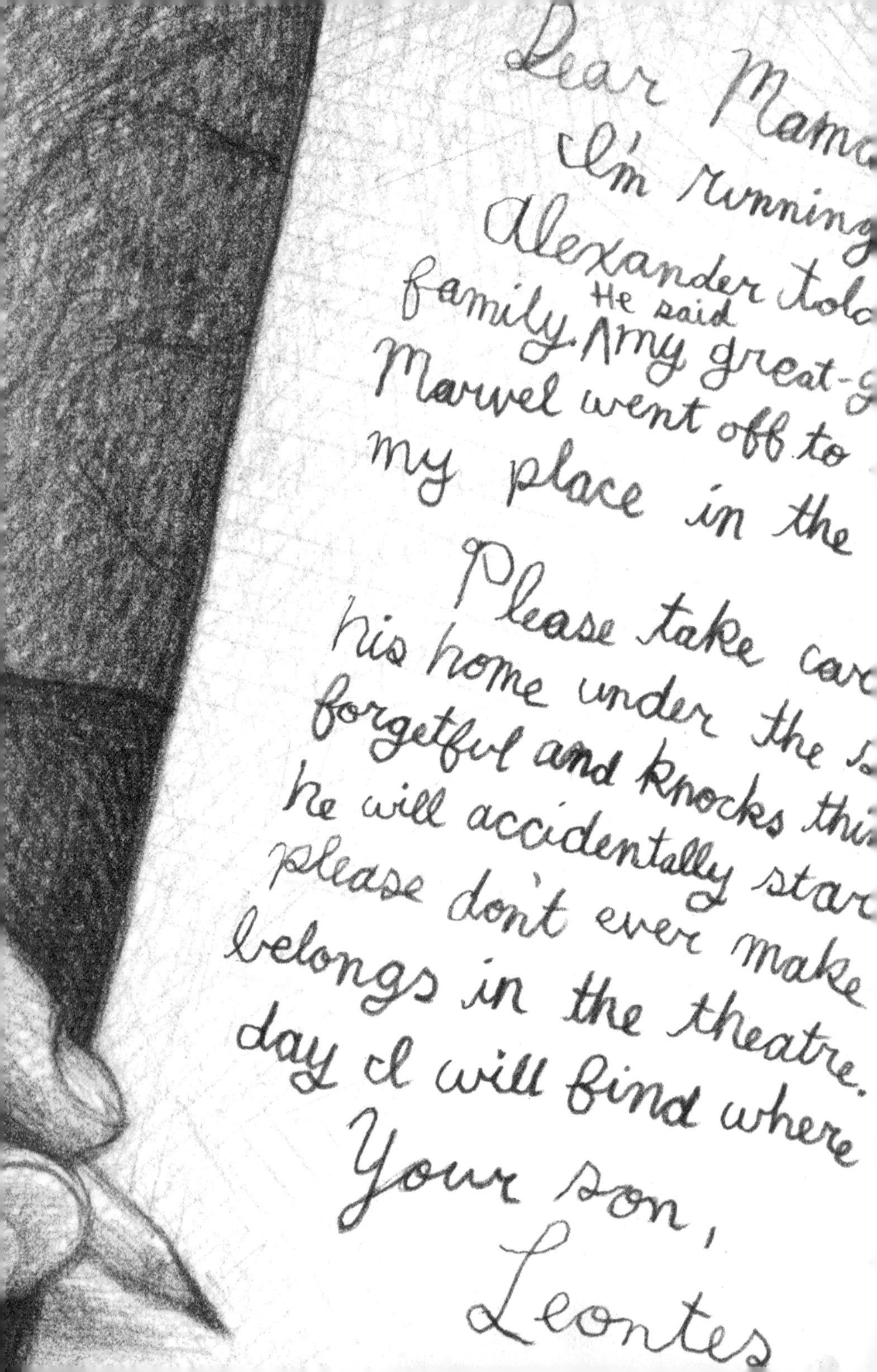

Dear Mama,
I'm running
Alexander told
He said
family. Amy great-g
Marvel went off to
my place in the

Please take car
his home under the s
forgetful and knocks thin
he will accidentally star
please don't ever make
belongs in the theatre.
day I will find where
Your son,
Leontes

10th January 1900

and Papa,

way. Grandfather

ne stories about our

t-grandfather Billy

a, and I need to find

orld too.

of grandfather in

ge. He's old and

over, I'm worried

a fire. But

im leave. He

I hope one

I belong too

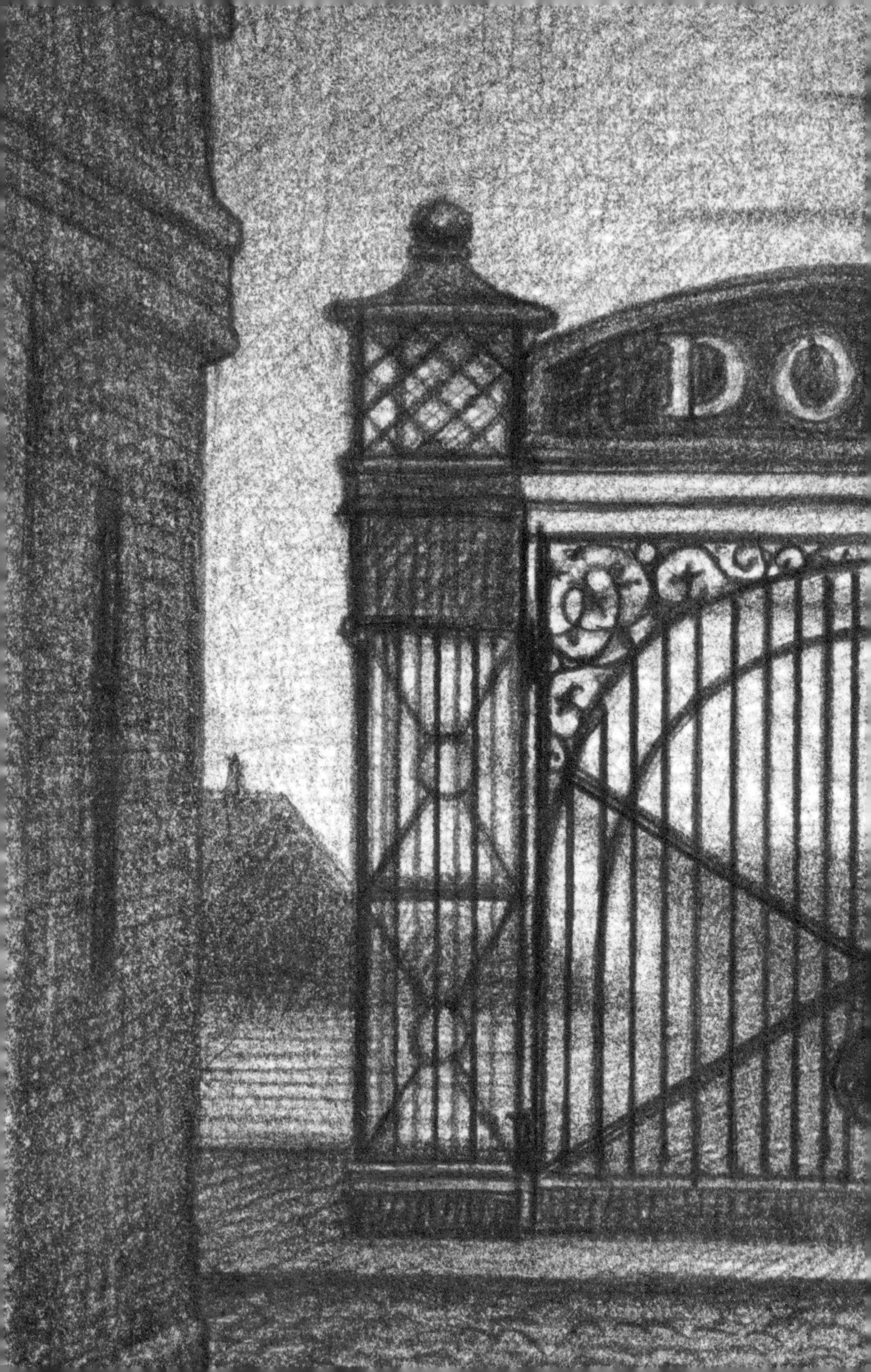
DO

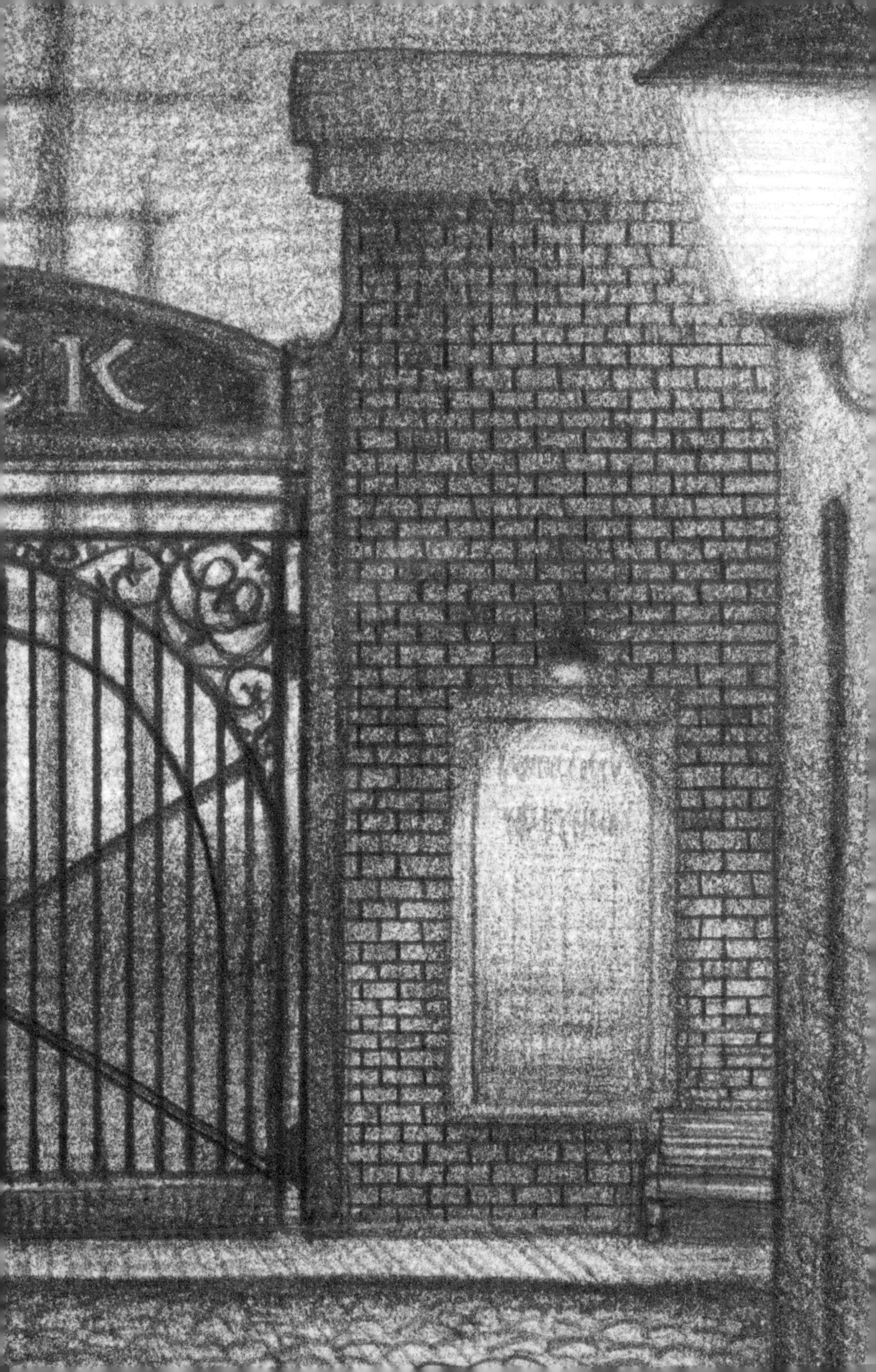

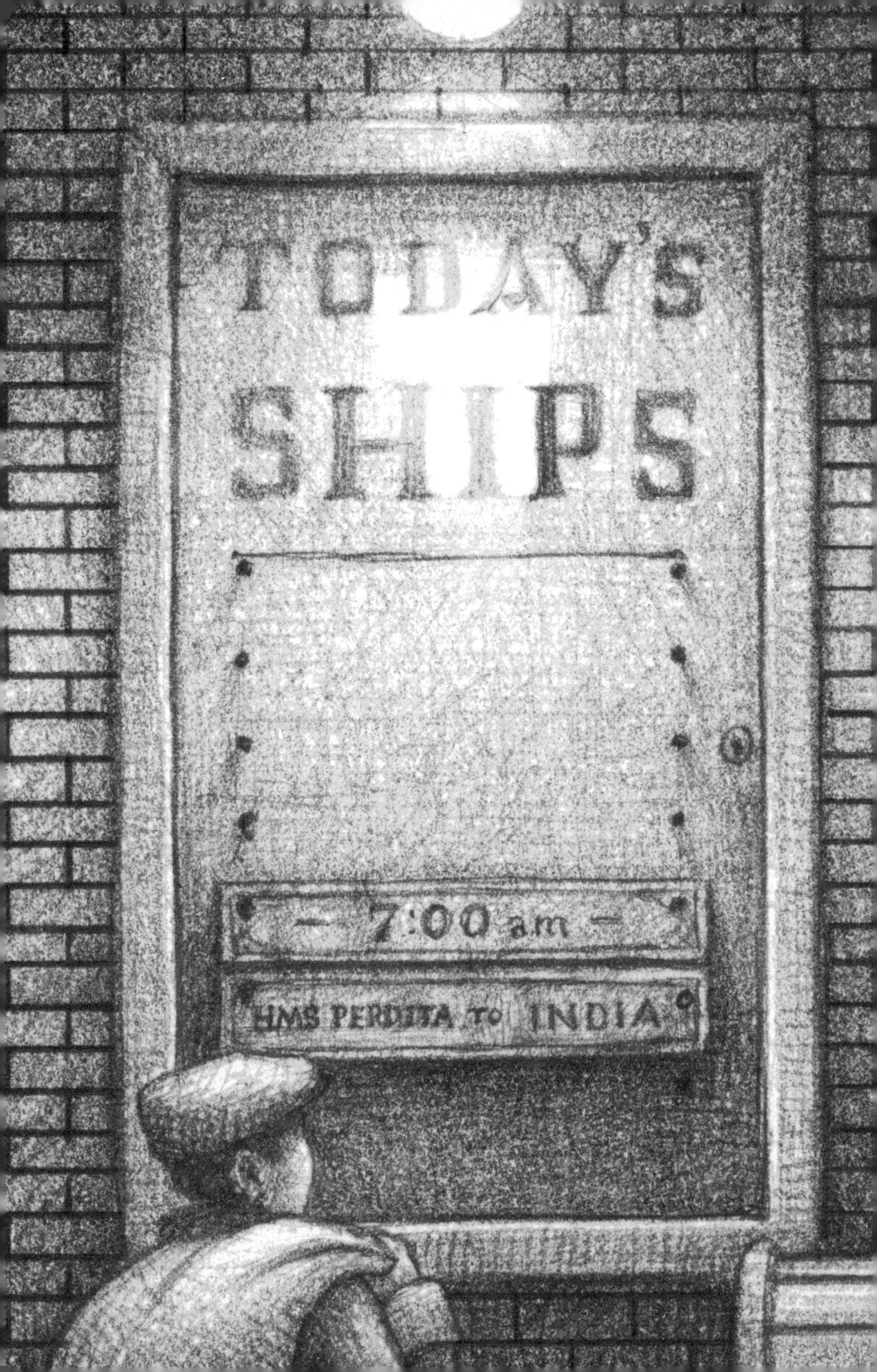
TODAY'S
SHIPS
7:00 am
HMS PERDITA TO INDIA

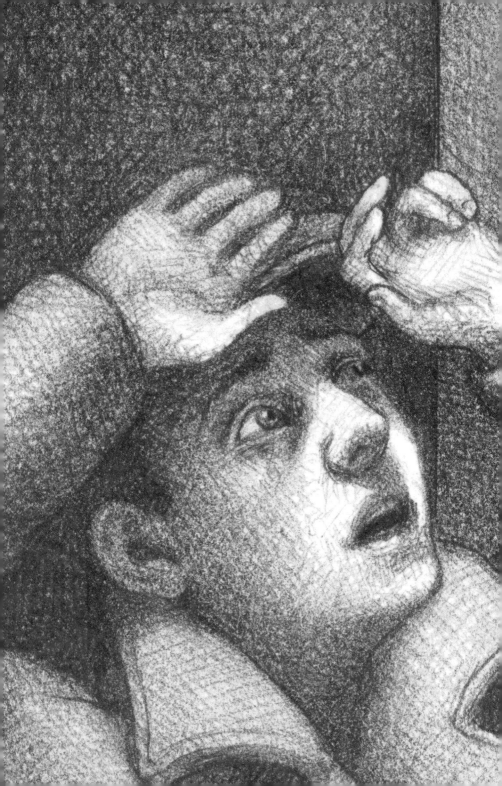

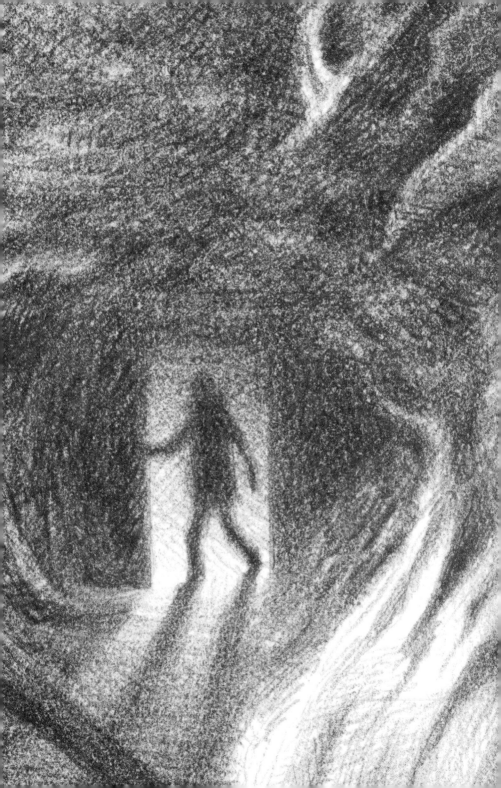

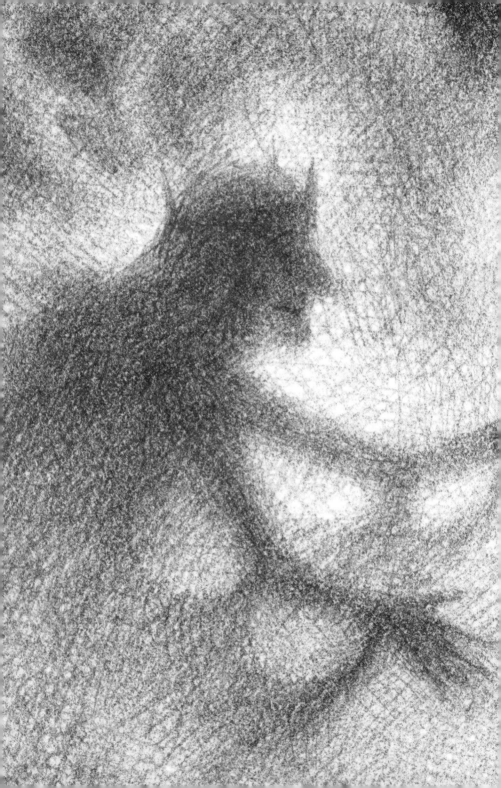

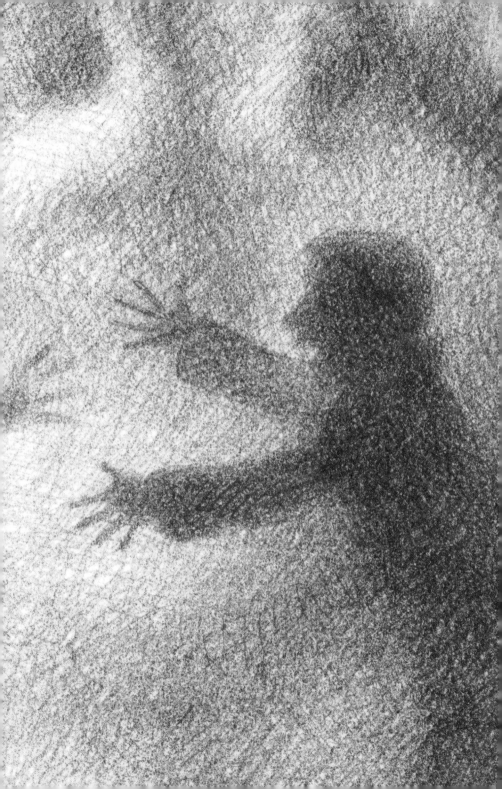

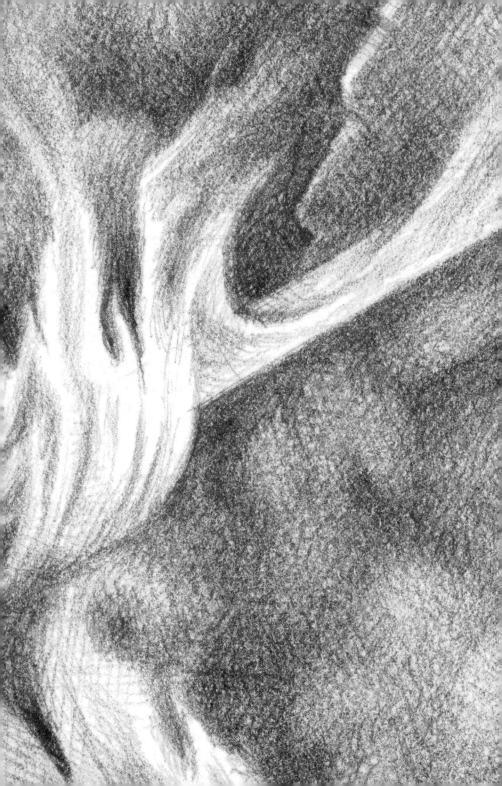

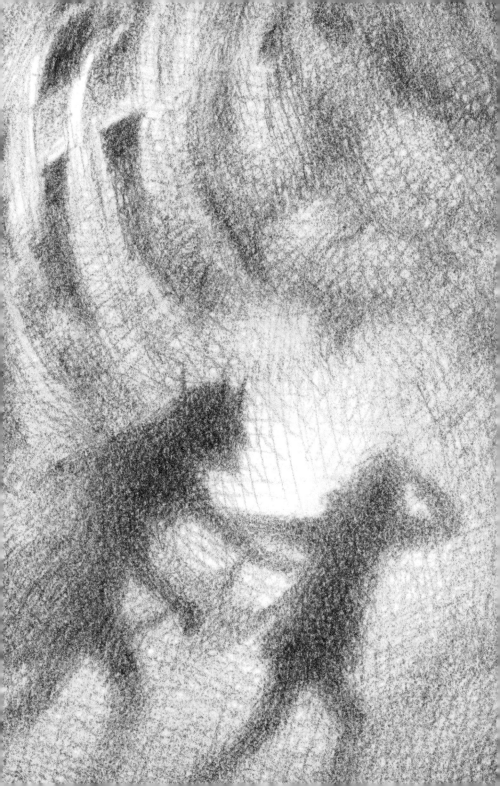

19

90

JOSEPH WAS LOST.

Somewhere far away the headlights of a car swept through the snowy night. He stopped to rest beneath a low passageway off an ancient cobblestone street. A single rusting streetlamp flickered nearby. He put down his heavy suitcase, dried off his glasses, and coughed. He was shocked he'd made it all the way to London without being caught. But then again, the headmaster at St. Anthony's was probably relieved he was gone.

Joseph leaned against the wall and pulled out the map he and Blink had made. They'd marked his uncle Albert's house at 18 Folgate Street with a big red X, as if they were looking for treasure. All Joseph knew about his uncle were a few overheard words from his mother through the years and the line in her address book: *A. Nightingale*, as if they were related to a bird. He had no idea what his uncle would say if he showed up unexpectedly at his house. He prayed A. Nightingale was a generous man, more generous than Joseph's parents, anyway, and he'd let Joseph stay for a few days and help him figure out how to track down Blink.

Joseph had forgotten his gloves on the train, and his hands were shaking. He couldn't make sense of the map at all.

If only he had run away with Blink when he'd had the chance, then he wouldn't be standing here alone and freezing. The hazy blue light made Joseph think of the nights the two of them would sneak off to some empty room at school, light a candle, and read out loud to each other from one of Blink's books. They'd quickly get caught up in the adventures of characters with names like Pip and Mowgli and Prince Caspian.

It was while reading *Kidnapped* by Robert Louis Stevenson that they first got the idea to run away together. Joseph knew it was just a game, but it was fun to imagine themselves on pirate ships or alone on desert islands. Soon their stories grew more complex. They dreamed of finding abandoned mansions in the woods and vanishing into secret chambers in ancient castles. Once, Joseph had mentioned he had an uncle in London he'd never met, and Blink insisted he get the address, just in case they were ever to really run away. Joseph had laughed, but as a surprise for Blink, he'd snuck into his mother's room during a visit home and copied down his uncle's address, which he proudly handed over when he returned to school.

That night, instead of reading together, the two boys had huddled in the library, creating a detailed map of the route that would lead them from St. Anthony's in Cornwall to Albert Nightingale's house in an area of London called Spitalfields, where their adventures would begin.

It was that same map Joseph was now holding, in the middle of a snowstorm, a couple of days after Christmas, lost in a city he didn't know. He was supposed to be here with Blink. But Blink was gone, leaving behind nothing except a single book, and Joseph had no idea if he'd ever see him again.

There was no one else Joseph could talk to about any of this, least of all his parents. They were always expressing concern that he spent too much time lost inside of stories, and now it seemed as if that's what actually had happened.

A dog barked in the distance, and the wind suddenly snatched the little map out of Joseph's shivering fingers. He picked up his suitcase and ran after it, towards a group of vagrants who were warming themselves over a fire by the side of the road. Joseph watched as the map was plucked out of the snow by one of the men, who looked at it briefly, turned it over, then crumpled it into a ball and fed it to the flames. Sparks lifted up from the fire like tiny orange insects, zigzagged into the air, and vanished.

Joseph panicked. What would he do without the map? He wondered if he should return to Liverpool Street Station and make his way back to school, but he'd already turned down so many streets and passed through so many little alleys, he wasn't sure he'd be able to even find the station again. And besides, the school probably wouldn't take him back now.

Joseph looked at his watch. It read 11:16.

The barking dog he'd heard before got louder, and suddenly a white blur came barrelling through the snow. It raced past him like a rock speeding down a mountainside.

A sound, high in the air, bounced off the brick walls and repeated itself.

"Marcus!"

Joseph, half-blinded by the snow and the darkness, turned a corner and ran straight into a boy who seemed to appear from nowhere. The boy was out of breath and his teeth were chattering. He was taller than Joseph, almost the same height as Blink, and he was wearing a blue cap.

"Hey!" gasped the boy. "Watch out!"

Joseph coughed.

"Have you seen Marcus?"

"Who?"

"My dog. He's white, so it's hard to find him in the snow. His name's *Marcus*."

Joseph adjusted his glasses and pointed down the street. "He ran that way."

The boy smiled and turned, but then stopped to look back. "You have a suitcase," he said. "Why do you have a suitcase? It's the middle of the night. And it's snowing!" The boy took a step closer. "Are you running away?"

"I'm looking for Folgate Street."

"That's right near my flat."

Joseph felt a wave of relief wash over him. "Fantastic!"

"But the only person who lives on Folgate Street is . . . wait . . . who are you looking for?"

"My uncle."

"Not . . . *Albert Nightingale*?"

"Yes! You know him?"

"Of course I know him! Everyone knows him. But . . ."

"But what?"

"Why does he *live* like that?"

"Like what?"

"You don't know?"

"Don't know *what*? I've never even met him. Please just tell me where he is! I'm freezing!"

"I'm freezing, too," said the boy. "I've been out here for hours looking for Snowball."

"Who's Snowball?"

"My dog!"

"How many dogs did you lose?"

The boy stared at Joseph. "What are you talking about?"

"You said your dog's name is Marcus."

"Oh! Right! No, I don't think that's it. It would upset my mum too much, and my dad probably wouldn't like it, either. Maybe Paddington!"

"Don't you know your own dog's name?"

"Not yet."

Joseph was confused, but he was distracted by the wind whipping down the street and the cold water seeping into his shoes. He looked again at his watch.

"What time is it?" asked the boy. "It must be late."

"I don't know."

"You just looked at your watch."

"It's broken."

"Then why did you look at it?"

Joseph's head was pounding. He didn't feel like talking; he just wanted to find his uncle.

"Why don't you get your watch fixed?" asked the boy.

"I don't *want* to get it fixed."

"Why not? What use is wearing a broken watch?"

Joseph wasn't about to tell this stranger the real

reason he wore the watch, and he was losing patience. *"What use is chasing a dog whose name you don't know?"* He turned and marched off down the street. He'd find his uncle's house on his own. It couldn't be too far now.

"Wait!" came a voice behind Joseph. "I'm sorry."

Joseph kept walking, but the boy jumped in front of him.

"What time is it?"

"Go away."

"Don't be so stroppy. I mean, what time is your watch *stuck at?*"

Joseph did not like this boy at all, but he pulled up his jacket sleeve and showed him the watch. "11:16. Now will you leave me alone?"

"I have an idea. Help me find my dog, and I'll help you find your uncle." The boy smiled.

Joseph sighed. "Do you promise?"

The boy nodded and adjusted his cap. His nose was bright red. "Good! Let's go!" He ran down the street shouting, "Pudding! Paddington!"

"How will we know when we get the name right?" asked Joseph, trying to keep up.

"When he answers to it!"

Joseph was tossed back into the labyrinth of ancient streets as he followed the boy, shouting the names of dogs from books he'd read: "Bull's-eye! Toto! Snowy! Pongo!" After a while they paused to catch their breath.

"Look," said the boy, pointing to a sign. "My father's shop."

The sign read BLOOM'S BAKERY.

A light was on in a window above the shop, and the shadow of a figure passed across the closed curtains. "And there's my dad! Keep your voice down."

"He doesn't know you're out here?"

The boy shook his head. "Do your parents know *you're* out here?"

Joseph's parents didn't really know *anything* about him. They lived their lives of great privilege, with their servants and their money and their travels that didn't include him. He glanced up at the window and changed the subject. "You live above a bakery?" he asked.

"No," the boy whispered.

"But—"

"Come on. This way!"

Soon a church steeple appeared in the distance, silhouetted against the moon, and the boys came to a long row of old brick buildings, all separated by a series of pitched glass roofs held up by cast-iron frames. The openings between the buildings led into a vast nighttime marketplace, lit by a procession of fluorescent lights.

Delivery trucks pulled in and out of the market, and inside were a hundred different stalls, with names like Gibbs and Pardoe Fruits, Great British Mushrooms, and David Kira, Banana Merchants. Old crates filled with fruits and vegetables were piled everywhere, and the place teemed with people, even at this hour. The boy pointed to a four-sided clock suspended from the ceiling in the centre of the market. It read 11:36.

"If we'd been here twenty minutes earlier," said the boy, "your watch would have been correct!"

A dizzying cascade of smells mingled in the cold air. People gathered for warmth around a cast-iron stove where someone was making tea. "The Little Drummer Boy" played on the radio. Christmas decorations still hung on the walls, and a few strings of coloured fairy lights blinked on and off, like a secret code.

Joseph and the boy ran up and down the aisles searching for the dog until they bumped into a man piling silvery fish onto ice. He wore a thick checked wool coat with a white apron tied over it, a long scarf, and a leather top hat.

"Frankie!" said the man, sounding surprised. "What are you doing here so late at night?" He spoke with a French accent, and there was a gap between his front teeth. "It's not the dog again, is it?"

Joseph noted the boy's name.

"Have you seen him?" asked Frankie, trying to catch his breath.

"Does your mother know you're out? You must not worry her so much."

"It's okay, she's asleep!"

"Sneaking around will only lead to trouble . . ."

Just then, there was movement at the end of a long aisle on the other side of the market. Someone shouted, "Get out of here, you runt!" They heard barking, and Joseph saw a dirty white ball of fur with something in its mouth dash out from beneath a table.

"Well, I think you have found your dog," the man in the top hat said with a curious smile.

Joseph and Frankie chased the dog into the streets again. After a few minutes, Joseph bent over to catch his breath, and he dropped his suitcase. It sprung open and as he looked down at his clothes and books in the snow, his glasses slid off his nose.

"Hello?" Joseph yelled. He found his glasses, dried them off, and put them back on. "Frankie?" There was no answer. "You promised you'd help me!"

Joseph returned everything to his suitcase, pausing when he came to the bright red book Blink had left behind. He carefully dried it off as much as possible and gently ran his hand along the cover. In gold letters, it read, *The Collected Poems of William Butler Yeats.* Joseph set it safely inside his suitcase.

Frankie was gone and Joseph's toes were going numb. He needed to find somewhere warm soon. He looked for an open doorway or a place he could escape from the snow for a little while. Finally, the howling wind took pity, and it spoke from far away.

"Follow the ship!"

It sounded like the beginning of a pirate adventure he and Blink would have loved. And then it came again . . .

"Follow the ship!"

Joseph realized it was Frankie's voice, calling to him from some other street.

"What are you talking about?" Joseph yelled into the night. "Where are you?"

But there was no answer now.

"What ship?" Joseph trembled. "Answer me!"

There was no ocean, no dock, nothing nearby at all, just streets and parked cars and darkness and snow.

Frankie's voice cut through the cold night air once more: *"Follow the ship!"*

Joseph looked up into the sky, although he wasn't sure why. Maybe he was looking for the moon, or a star, or a chimney with plumes of smoke to guide himself by.

He thought he saw something far away glint in the dark. He cleaned off his glasses to get a better look and found himself walking towards a mysterious glow.

And there it was.

Appearing through the snow, high in the air, was a golden sailing ship, like a dream a lost sailor might have. Joseph thought of "The Little Match Girl," a story he'd read in school last year about a girl who ended up dead in the snow after a freezing night filled with beautiful visions. Joseph hoped he wasn't imagining the golden ship, and he prayed his own story wouldn't turn out like the Little Match Girl's.

Not knowing what else to do, Joseph ran towards the ship. As he drew nearer, he saw it was a massive golden weather vane, signalling to him. A sign that read FOLGATE STREET was just visible beneath a thin sheen of snow on the corner, and soon he was standing in front of an old brick building in the middle of the dark narrow road. There was a large metal gas lamp hanging above the entrance, illuminating a brass knocker shaped like the head of a dog with a ring in its mouth. Pine garlands with red velvet ribbons were hung around the doorframe. The house provided the only light on all of Folgate Street.

The number 18 was nailed to the centre of the door.

JOSEPH STOOD ON his toes and looked through one of the glowing windows.

A magnificent fire burned brightly in a fireplace, and a sparkling chandelier ringed with candles hung from the ceiling. On a shiny black table beneath the chandelier were tall, glimmering white tapers, a pair of silver pitchers, a few sets of crystal goblets, and the half-eaten remains of a lavish dinner. On the wall above the mantel, presiding over everything, was an old painting, in an ornate gold frame, of a dark-eyed man. Heavy velvet curtains hung on either side of the window, like the curtains in a theatre. Joseph felt as if someone had taken a pair of scissors and cut into the fabric of the street, pulling it back to reveal a hidden nineteenth-century world, waiting just beneath the freezing twentieth-century surface.

It was better than anything he or Blink could have imagined, and for a brief, bizarre moment, Joseph thought he might have *actually* fallen back in time, or stumbled upon a portal to the past. Of course, he knew that was impossible . . . time travel wasn't real; it only existed in books and movies. But he'd never seen anything like this before. And he'd never *felt* anything like it, either. The closest he could think of was when he and Blink were immersed in a book together. Sometimes a strange feeling would come over them as they'd race through the pages, and the words would dissolve, and they'd find themselves deep inside Oz, or Narnia, or the Andes, or Africa, where everything was real and vivid and alive.

Stories could do that, but this wasn't a story. This was a *house*. And no matter how real a story seemed, you still couldn't eat the food, or pick up the plates, or warm yourself by the fire.

There was movement through the thick glass, and someone appeared at the far end of the room. The person seemed to float in the golden light, like an undersea creature caught in the tide. The figure turned towards the window, and a wave of fear washed over Joseph. He quickly ducked out of view.

When he caught his breath and peeked again, the person had disappeared. Minutes later the front door swung open. Joseph dashed behind an abandoned car across the street.

The man in the doorway did not look friendly. He was thin and bearded and seemed to be scowling. He wore leather gloves and some kind of heavy canvas apron beneath an open fur coat that stretched down to his ankles. Joseph had never seen a man in a fur coat before. A purple hat sat crookedly on his head, and a white pipe was clamped between his teeth. He was holding a bright red snow shovel.

Joseph couldn't believe this strange man was related to his mother. Maybe he had the wrong house. His mother was endlessly concerned with being *proper* and worried about things Joseph couldn't understand, like parties, and guest lists, and looking presentable. How could her brother be wearing a purple hat and a fur coat? This man seemed to be from a different universe than Joseph's mother.

The man looked both ways as if to make sure the coast was clear, then stepped outside into the freezing cold and started shovelling his way down the pavement.

The white dog reappeared in the distance, heading in his direction, followed closely by Frankie. Before Joseph could move, the dog jumped into his lap and licked him as if they were old friends.

Frankie mouthed the words "Hold him!" as he snuck up and leapt forwards. "Got you!"

The boy grasped the barking animal, and Joseph pulled them both down behind the car just as the man shovelling snow turned around.

"Bad runaway!" said Frankie, and for a second Joseph wasn't sure if he was talking to him or the dog. "Thanks for helping me catch him!"

"You need to get a collar and lead for your dog," Joseph whispered.

"To tell you the truth, he's not really my dog."

"What?"

"I mean, not yet . . . he's a stray. I've been chasing him for a while. I'm going to adopt him. I don't want him to freeze to death out here!"

"Please just go away."

"Why are we whispering? That's Albert Nightingale right there. I thought you were *looking* for him." Frankie, trying to hold on to the struggling dog, lost his footing and fell backwards in the slippery snow. The dog immediately leapt from his arms and disappeared down the street again. "No! Oliver! Sunshine! Come back!"

"Now will you leave me alone?" whispered Joseph.

"You're as strange as your uncle!" Frankie hissed. "If my dog gets hit by a car or freezes to death, it's going to be your fault!"

"How is it my fault? He's not even your dog!"

"Oh, sod off!" Frankie sneered at him as he rushed after the dog.

Joseph shook his head. He hoped he'd never see that boy, or that dog, again. He dried his glasses, took a breath, and looked at his broken watch.

The time had come.

With his suitcase tucked tightly under his arm, he ran up behind his uncle and tapped him on the shoulder. The fur on his coat was soft and his pipe smoke smelled sweet. The man turned.

Joseph stared up into his uncle's glittering green eyes.

His uncle stared right back. "Yes?" he said, after it became clear Joseph wasn't going to speak first.

Joseph shook himself as if he was coming out of a dream. "Albert Nightingale?"

The man took a long drag on his pipe, exhaled, and said, "Who wants to know?"

"I'm Joseph . . . sir."

The man's eyes widened, but he didn't say anything.

"Joseph *Jervis*," said Joseph. "Your nephew?" He pulled off his hat, revealing red hair that fell down over his forehead, almost to his eyes. "See, like my mum. And you."

The man studied him and scratched his beard, which was the exact same shade of red as Joseph's hair.

"Put your hat back on," he said in a low grumble. "And stop calling me *sir*. You look like you're getting sick."

Albert Nightingale took off a glove, and Joseph flinched, thinking he was going to slap him with it, but he placed his cool palm against Joseph's burning forehead. Then he felt Joseph's cheek with the back of his hand.

"I'm fine." Joseph put his hat back on and tried not to cough.

"You're so big."

No one had ever called Joseph big. He was shorter than most of his classmates, and he was too skinny, according to the grown-ups he knew. "I'm thirteen."

"So that was you looking in the window before, and hiding behind the car over there with Frankie?"

"You saw us?"

"Hard to miss you with that awful dog barking so much." Albert stared at Joseph and puffed on his pipe. His accent was American, like Joseph's mother's, but sometimes he pronounced things the English way, so his speech sounded rather mixed up, as though he didn't come from anywhere. People sometimes told Joseph his own accent was hard to place, since it was partly English and partly American, and had hints of the other places he'd lived, like Switzerland and the Middle East.

"What are you doing here?"

"Looking for you."

"Does your mother know you're here?"

Joseph shook his head. "Can I stay here? With you? Please?"

Albert Nightingale laughed, but it wasn't a friendly laugh. "Your parents have moved back to London, I assume?"

"No."

"No? Then how . . ." Albert wiped his hand across his face and sighed. "Last I heard, your father was running a bank in China."

"My parents are in Germany now. After Saudi Arabia and Hong Kong."

"So how in the world did you get *here*? Did you stow away on some ship in the middle of the night?"

Joseph imagined being a stowaway and wished it was true. "No . . . I just got to London by train a few hours ago."

"From where?"

"School." Joseph shivered and looked up into his uncle's flashing eyes.

"Does *anyone* know where you are?"

"You do."

"Good god, Joseph, everyone must be worried sick."

Joseph doubted that.

Albert looked up into the sky, then back at Joseph. "You can't stay here."

"But . . . I have nowhere else to go."

"That can't possibly be true. Doesn't your father have family in London?'"

"No."

"Then where are they?'"

"Can't I stay for a few days? You don't have to tell anyone." Joseph's voice cracked.

"Joseph . . . you can't just . . ."

"What's wrong? What?" Joseph started coughing again.

Albert shook his head. "Listen to me. Go inside and leave your shoes by the door. Then head straight up to the top floor, to the room with the green door. Take off your wet clothes, lay them by the fire. Change into something dry, and warm yourself up. When I'm done out here, I'll bring you some aspirin and hot tea. Can you do that?'"

Joseph was elated. "So I *can* stay?'"

"No, Joseph, you *can't* stay. You're just going up there to dry off. I don't need you getting pneumonia while I figure out what to do with you."

Joseph stepped into the house and looked back at his uncle.

"Don't touch anything," his uncle warned.

Joseph coughed and closed the door behind him.

THE MODERN WORLD vanished along with the cold air as the smell of fire and food overwhelmed him. There was a delicious pine smell, too, from the Christmas garlands that were hung all down the hall.

Joseph's skin felt prickly. He removed his shoes and set them by the door. A small framed painting hung to his right. Even in the dark, Joseph could see it was a painting of a shipwreck. A single word was barely legible on the frame, written by hand in black ink: *Kraken.*

Joseph had learned something about shipwrecks as a pupil at St. Anthony's, which was named after the patron saint of shipwrecks and lost things. Exhausted and wet, he felt like the survivor of a shipwreck himself, a lost boy who'd just washed up on the doorstep of his uncle's mysterious house.

At the end of the hallway was the staircase Uncle Albert had told him to climb. But to his right, just beyond the painted shipwreck, were shiny black double doors that opened into the dining room he'd seen from the street. Inside, the fire hissed and snapped and cast flickering shadows across the glossy green walls. Joseph couldn't help himself. Mesmerized, he put down his suitcase and felt himself pulled into the room, like a moth fluttering helplessly towards the light.

He'd never been in a warmer or more wonderful place in his life. It was as if he really had tumbled headfirst into a book of fairy stories, and all he wanted to do was share it with Blink.

Joseph went to the table. Forks and knives had been set down on the dirty plates, and drinks were half-drunk. Chairs were pushed back haphazardly, and Joseph wondered for a moment if he'd interrupted a supper party. But no one was around. It was the strangest thing, as if everyone had just suddenly vanished.

Joseph wasn't really hungry but he hadn't eaten since breakfast, so he forced down a few nuts and snatched a small slice of bread. He spotted a napkin on the floor next to a chair and placed it back on the table. He took a drink from a glass filled with something clear. It was too late before he realized it definitely was not water and choked. He drank from another glass, but it was wine and tasted even worse. The man in the antique painting above the fireplace stared down at him disapprovingly.

Joseph moved closer to the fire to warm his hands and noticed, for the first time, that the man had red hair.

A bird's shrill whistle interrupted the quiet. Joseph

glanced up to see a birdcage by the window, but there was no bird in the cage. Perhaps it had escaped and was hiding in one of the dark corners of the room, or maybe Joseph's fever was causing him to hallucinate. He thought he'd better get upstairs before his uncle came in. He stumbled out to the hallway, picked up his suitcase, and leaned for a moment against a tall old clock.

At the foot of the dark wooden staircase, Joseph noticed another black door open just a crack, nearly hidden in the shadows. He peeked inside. A Christmas tree stood in the corner, its tin star brushing the ceiling. An antique piano, topped with lace and weighed down with a thousand little knickknacks, sat against a wall. A doll in a red velvet dress and a wooden truck had been tossed aside by some children. Two open boxes and ripped Christmas paper lay on the floor nearby.

Children?

It had never occurred to Joseph that his uncle might have a family. He felt a sense of relief as he imagined meeting his aunt and cousins in the morning. Maybe they'd help win over his uncle. He wondered how old his cousins were, and which rooms they were sleeping in, and whether they had red hair, too. Why had no one ever mentioned them?

Just then, one of the boxes at Joseph's feet moved by

itself. He leaned over to look closer, and a black cat leapt out and darted up the stairs. Joseph nearly dropped his suitcase.

With his head growing dizzier, Joseph shut the door behind him and climbed up the stairs. His heartbeat thumped in his ears with every step. He gripped the smooth bannister to steady himself. His cousins had left more toys scattered on the stairs: a wooden mouse, a toy theatre, some paper dolls. He stepped carefully over everything. The doors on the next landing were closed, and he tiptoed so he wouldn't wake anyone up. Somehow he felt comforted knowing there were other people living here, too.

Candles on the window ledges lit his way and he noticed all the different smells . . . strange spices, extinguished fires and burning cedar, sweets, powders, and perfumes.

On the last set of stairs to the top floor, Joseph ducked beneath faded, tattered laundry that hung from lines like ghosts. In the corner of the landing was a steep set of steps, sort of like a ladder, covered almost completely with boxes and old bolts of fabric, that must have led up to an attic. In front of him was the green door his uncle had told him about. The paint was chipped and it stood half-open, beckoning him inside. Joseph silently entered, as if he was under a spell.

The room was dominated by a giant decaying bed decorated with huge posts at each corner, dusty velvet curtains hanging from above, and black tassels and carved gargoyles covered in cobwebs. The room smelled like dust and smoke. Joseph put down his suitcase and looked around.

In the far corner, a tall desk was wedged into an alcove between a bookcase and a window. It was piled high with books and papers, along with an old brass clock, a small bust of Shakespeare, and some half-used candles in candleholders. A fireplace opposite the bed roared with a warm and inviting fire, and a memory came to him of a strange, dreamlike week visiting his grandfather in America when he was six. Blink was the only person he'd ever shared this memory with. His grandfather had been very kind to him, reading Joseph stories from old books in front of a fireplace in a room filled with statues and boxes and who knew what else. They stayed up late and made something in the fire called s'mores with marshmallows on sticks. They were delicious, but it was the flames that transfixed him. One morning, when Joseph was exploring the room by himself, he found a broken watch and his grandfather surprised him by letting him keep it.

After the visit, Joseph had returned with his parents to their home in the deserts of Saudi Arabia, and within a few months, his grandfather died of a heart attack. Joseph put on the broken watch and decided to re-create the beloved study he remembered from America. Since there was no fireplace in Joseph's playroom, he turned over his toy chest and stuffed it with newspapers. Matches were easy to find because both his parents smoked, and soon he had a fire going. The flames were so beautiful to look at. He thought about his grandfather, and how nice he'd been, and Joseph wondered what happened to people after they died.

The flames grew and soon his mother smelled the smoke and rushed in. She went nearly out of her mind with anger when she saw what Joseph had done. After the screaming and spanking subsided, Joseph's parents forced him to say he was sorry, especially about the expensive Persian rug he'd destroyed. He wasn't really sorry, though. He had done it to remember his grandfather, and he loved the flames. But his parents didn't understand. They wouldn't even listen to him as he tried to explain. They just packed him off to the boarding school in Switzerland soon afterwards.

He was the youngest boy the school had ever taken.

JOSEPH RUBBED HIS sweating forehead. He took off his wet shoes and socks. The clothes inside his suitcase were wet, too, and his books were damp, so he carefully placed everything in front of the fire. He'd brought six of his favourite books: *Great Expectations*, *Kidnapped*, *The Witches*, *A Wrinkle in Time*, *The Hitchhiker's Guide to the Galaxy*, and of course Blink's red book of poetry. He quickly read his favourite poem, the one his friend had underlined, and then set the book by the fire to dry with the others.

Unsure what to do next, he opened a cupboard door next to the fireplace. A strange but appealingly musty smell enveloped him. Old-fashioned velvet jackets and white shirts hung from silk hangers, and formal trousers and more shirts were folded neatly in drawers. The clothes seemed to be around Joseph's size. He found a long white cotton nightshirt with nice pearly buttons. He took off his clothes and slipped it on. Then he pulled out a folded blanket and wrapped it around himself. The giant velvet bed looked very inviting now, but he thought he should wait up for his uncle.

Above the fireplace on a wooden shelf was a beautiful, dusty model ship, its sails billowing in an imaginary wind. Joseph went to inspect it. The name of the vessel was written on the side in tiny white letters that had mostly flaked off. But the first letters looked like Kr, and Joseph wondered if this was the same ship that had sunk in the painting downstairs. Maybe his uncle was a naval historian or a sailor. Joseph ran his fingers over the smooth crystal of his watch. 11:16. The gold face glinted brightly in the firelight, and Joseph wished once again that Blink was with him.

The two of them had met a year earlier, in the library at school. Joseph was reading when a distant clicking noise had caused him to look up. Across the room was a dark-haired boy he hadn't seen before. The boy tapped his fingers against the table and winked, which made Joseph blush. But then he realized this must be the new student everyone was talking about, the one who twitched. Some of the boys said he'd been electrocuted, because his fingers twitched and so did his head and his legs and his eyes. It was hard not to stare at his involuntary movements, but Joseph smiled at the boy, and the boy adjusted the tie of his school uniform and smiled right back. Then he closed his book, put it under his arm, and walked over to Joseph. He seemed very tall.

"What's your name?" the boy asked, extending his hand.

"I'm Joseph." For some reason he became nervous. He could feel a slight tremor in the boy's hand when they touched.

"Call me Blink."

Joseph wasn't sure he'd heard correctly. *"Blink?"*

The boy nodded, and twitched, and blinked. "It's a nickname I made up. Can you guess why?"

"Because . . . you blink?"

The boy smiled. "Right! And it shows I'm not ashamed of it. Sometimes people say mean things, and I want them to know I don't care. Plus, I think it's a good name, don't you?"

"Yes, it is. A good name, I mean."

"And there's probably not a lot of other boys named Blink at this school, I'm guessing."

Joseph laughed. He was impressed with the boy right away, but he wasn't sure what to ask next. He stood up, too. "Um, does it hurt?"

"The nickname?" A quick smile showed the boy was joking.

"Sorry, stupid question."

"At least you didn't ask me if I was electrocuted. I get that all the time. It doesn't hurt, by the way. It's just annoying sometimes. But when I'm concentrating really hard on something, like playing the violin, or reading, it calms down." Blink showed Joseph the book he was reading. It was a bright red paperback. *The Collected Poems of William Butler Yeats.* "You know his poems?"

Joseph was embarrassed. "No."

"Listen to this." Blink flipped through the pages and read one out loud. It began, *Had I the heavens' embroidered cloths, Enwrought with golden and silver light.*

Joseph had no idea what the poem meant, but the words were beautiful and they sat down together to read it again.

Blink eventually noticed Joseph glancing at his broken watch. "Sorry," said Joseph. "It's a weird habit. I look at it all the time, even though it always says 11:16. My grandfather gave it to me when I was little. I guess I should fix it."

"No! Don't!"

"Why not?"

"Even a broken watch is correct twice a day." Blink disappeared into the shelves for a moment before returning with an encyclopedia. He set it on the table and opened it. He pointed to a photograph of a piece of amber the colour of honey. Frozen inside the gemstone was an ancient insect, stuck forever. "Maybe time is like that insect," Blink said, "trapped beneath the crystal of your watch."

Joseph knew at that moment he and Blink were going to be friends.

Church bells in the distance roused Joseph out of his memory. The fire in the dusty room was warm, but he could still feel a cold breeze coming in through a crack in the wall. He pulled the blanket tighter around himself and thought about the question Frankie had asked him earlier that night: *"Why does your uncle live like that?"*

Maybe Uncle Albert's time had got stuck, too. Maybe that's why the house, and everything in it, was so old. Maybe trouble with time ran in their family.

JOSEPH'S MIND CONTINUED to race as he waited for his uncle to appear. He ran his hand along the dusty mantel beneath the model ship, where a few items were scattered about . . . a miniature copper pitcher, an oyster shell, an empty glass jar, and a small leather case, about the size of his palm, embossed with flowers. A little metal clasp shaped like a sliver of the moon held the case shut. Curious, he carefully slipped it open.

Inside was an old black-and-white photograph of a boy, about Joseph's age, with sad eyes that stared straight at him. The boy was seated on a chair, a striped tie was folded at his neck, and his short hair was parted to one side, with a few stray pieces sticking up.

Someone had hand-coloured the boy's hair.

It was red.

On the left side of the case on yellowing paper was a tiny pencil sketch of a beautiful angel, his wings outstretched. In one hand the angel held a sword and in the other, a lantern.

The drawing was signed at the bottom: *Leo.*

Was this Leo's room? Was Joseph wearing Leo's

nightshirt? His head throbbed and he sat on the bed. The mattress wasn't as hard as he'd imagined, and he lay back, still wrapped in the blanket from the cupboard. The room spun.

Joseph tried to focus on the drawing of the angel and on Leo. Was it his imagination or did he hear whispering in other rooms, footsteps walking back and forth, and the clip-clop of horses on the street outside? More bells seemed to ring from somewhere far away. Joseph wanted to get up and look out the window, but for some reason he was sure the streets would be empty. There would be no horses. It was as if the world was full of ghosts.

He thought he heard footsteps on the stairs, but his uncle didn't appear. He closed the leather case and clutched it to his chest. As he drifted off to sleep, he could still see the steady fire across the room. Someone's voice seemed to call to him, and soon he found himself in the arms of an angel, floating high above a burning city.

JOSEPH OPENED HIS eyes. Moonlight flooded through the windows. All the candles in the room had been blown out and the fire reduced to ash. It was colder now, but another blanket had been placed on top of him and tucked in tightly, outlining his body like a mummy. His glasses sat on a table by the bed, next to a glass of water and an empty teacup. He had a vague memory of his uncle bringing him pills earlier and helping him downstairs to the lavatory, which was hidden behind the panelling in the cellar. His head still hurt, and his skin felt hot. The house was strangely quiet.

A shadow spread across the room, and Joseph turned.

Standing in the doorway, as if summoned from his dreams, was a ghost.

Joseph screamed.

In that instant, the spirit dissolved, and a moment later Albert Nightingale, wrapped in a long green dressing gown, came bursting into the room.

"Joseph! What happened?"

"The boy!"

"What boy?"

"The one from the photograph. Leo! He was here!"

"You scared me. It's your fever. You were having a dream."

"I was awake. I just saw him." Joseph realized the leather case was no longer in his hands. "Where's the photo? Give it to me."

"It's back on the mantel, where it belongs."

Joseph coughed and tried to sit up. His uncle eased him back down and sat next to him on the bed. He gave Joseph two more aspirin.

"Who is he?" asked Joseph.

"Who?"

"The boy in the photograph, the one with the red hair. *Leo.*"

"It's no one, Joseph."

"He's here, in the house! Is he related to us?"

"Enough. Shut your eyes. We'll talk in the morning."

Joseph felt hot and cold at the same time, and half-crazed. "The angel came to me in my dream."

Albert stared at his nephew for a few moments and brushed the sweaty hair from his eyes.

Just then, there was a small metallic crash from upstairs, and they both looked towards the attic. "It's Leo," said Joseph.

"It's Madge."

"Who's that?"

"The cat. Now go back to sleep."

Albert said something else, but the words were lost to Joseph as a ghostly voice called to him from the attic, and the angel reappeared with outspread wings above an ocean made of fire.

"BLINK!" SHOUTED JOSEPH as he woke up from his dream.

Someone was in the room, and in his confusion, Joseph thought it was the ghost again. He put on his glasses and his uncle snapped into focus. They locked eyes for a moment. His uncle's red hair was brushed to the side and his beard was neatly trimmed. He wore the same canvas apron around his waist that he'd had on the night before and keys jangled at his side. He looked like he'd been up for hours. There was a tray with bread and jam and hot tea next to the bed, but Joseph couldn't imagine eating anything right now.

Albert puffed on his pipe and tended the fire in the fireplace. Then he picked up one of Joseph's books from the floor. Joseph saw the flash of a red cover.

"Do you always travel with a library?" he asked. Albert placed the book, along with the others, into Joseph's suitcase. He then began to fold Joseph's clothes and place them into the suitcase, too.

"What are you doing?" Joseph asked through a fog.

"Packing."

"Why?"

"You can't stay here."

"Where are you going to send me?"

"I don't know."

"Please! No!" Joseph felt nauseous and his head pounded. He closed his eyes and coughed. "I'm so dizzy."

"You're *hungover*! I saw what you drank last night. Aren't you a little young for alcohol?"

"I . . . I thought it was water . . ."

"And you moved a napkin."

"A napkin?"

"I told you not to touch anything, Joseph."

"The napkin that was on the floor? I was trying to be helpful."

"Ah."

Joseph coughed again and wiped the sweaty hair from his eyes. "I had such strange dreams last night . . ."

Albert, the pipe clamped in his teeth, continued to fold Joseph's clothes and put them in his suitcase.

"Stop!" said Joseph, as loudly as he could.

Albert looked up and raised an eyebrow.

"Does your wife know I'm here?" Joseph said desperately. "Maybe she'll want me to stay. Maybe she'll tell me what's going on!"

"I'm sorry, *what*?"

"Where are they?"

"*Who?*"

"Your wife and kids. I want to meet them!"

"My wife?"

"And kids."

"I don't have a wife and kids."

"You don't? Then . . . who else lives here?"

"I live alone, Joseph."

At that moment, the cat crept through the door and wound herself between Albert's legs. "Well, I live alone with Madge." He picked up the cat and placed her on his shoulders. She sat there for a moment, then jumped off and disappeared. "Has your mother really never told you *anything* about me?"

Joseph shook his head. "No," he said, almost silently.

Albert leaned against a wall near the bed and covered his eyes. He tugged on a small round medallion that was suspended from a silver chain around his neck. When he spoke again, he sounded like he was talking more to himself than to Joseph. "I shouldn't have let you stay last night. I was going to ring your parents right away, I really was, and insist they send someone to come get you immediately, but I didn't have their phone number, and you looked so sick. And when I came upstairs you'd fallen asleep, and . . ."

"I knew it!"

Albert looked warily at his nephew. "Knew what?"

"When I finally found your house last night . . . I looked in the window, and I saw that it was . . ." He stopped to search for just the right word.

"It was what?" said Albert, impatiently.

"It was . . . beautiful."

Albert shifted and his eyes briefly softened, but then he said, "Enough."

"I knew you'd let me stay."

"I'm not letting you stay. I talked to your headmaster this morning."

"How do you know where I go to *school*?"

"What do you think, Joseph? I went through your things. You have a suitcase full of books from the library at St. Anthony's, and a school uniform with the name embroidered on the pocket. The headmaster told me your parents are on a cruise somewhere unreachable."

Joseph felt a strange combination of joy and terror, but he didn't say a word.

Albert slowly moved closer to Joseph's bed. The medallion around his neck glinted in the morning light.

"Your headmaster was very angry."

Joseph's head was spinning, and a long tense silence settled across the room.

"You set *fires*, Joseph?" Albert's voice was low and dangerous.

"No! It was an *accident*! I swear!"

Albert laughed an unpleasant laugh. "My entire house is flammable, and it's filled with fireplaces and candles, and *that's* supposed to make me feel better?"

"You don't understand! I like fire!"

"That makes it *worse*, Joseph!"

"No! Listen to me. When I was little, my mother took me to visit my grandfather in America, and he had a fireplace."

"I'm aware, Joseph. He was my father, too."

"Right, well, we didn't have fireplaces in Saudi Arabia. He read to me at night by the fire. I loved the stories. When he died, I was so sad." And then Joseph told Albert about making the fire in his toy chest, and burning the Persian rug, and being sent away to boarding school, and how he'd been fascinated by fire ever since. "That's why I loved reading with Blink by candlelight at night, and—"

"*Blink?* Who's Blink?"

"My best mate! That's his nickname."

Albert sat on a chair beside the bed, close enough that Joseph could now see the silver medallion around his neck . . . a bird with outstretched wings. "Your headmaster said you set fire to your *desk* yesterday."

"I was writing a letter to Blink," said Joseph. "I felt sick, so I put my head down on the desk. When I woke up, I smelled smoke. I thought it was a dream, but my eyes were open and the letter was *on fire*, right in front of me. The candle must have fallen over. *It was an accident.* I jumped up and put out the flames with a blanket. But I knew this was a disaster. My parents were going to kill me. And . . ."

"That's enough, Joseph."

"You don't understand. Blink's father showed up unexpectedly a couple months ago. Blink came running into my room and begged me to run away with him, but I was too scared. Now Blink's gone, and I have to find him! I need your help. That's why I'm here! You're the only person who can help me. I had the map we made to your house and—"

"You had a *map* to my house?"

"Blink and I, well, it's a long story, but I—"

"Stop talking, Joseph. You still have a fever."

"I'm fine. Do you—"

"Just promise me you won't burn down my house."

Albert's face was like stone, and he didn't take his eyes off of Joseph. *"I said, promise me you won't burn down my house."*

Joseph was sweating and his ears began to ring. His

eyelids felt heavy and he could still smell the smoke from the burning letter. Of course, he didn't have Blink's address, so there was nowhere to send it, but it had been comforting to write it somehow. He'd said *"Happy Christmas"* and *"I miss you."* And he'd told Blink about being left behind at school. *"My parents told me they had some travelling to do so I can't come home for the holidays. The kids who are left behind are still called The Unwanteds, but it's less fun when you're not with me."*

And at the end of the letter, Joseph added, *"P.S. After you left, I found your copy of the Yeats book, and I saw you underlined one of the poems. It was the first poem you read to me. Do you remember? I keep wondering if you underlined it just for me."*

> *Had I the heavens' embroidered cloths,*
> *Enwrought with golden and silver light,*
> *The blue and the dim and the dark cloths*
> *Of night and light and the half light,*
> *I would spread the cloths under your feet:*
> *But I, being poor, have only my dreams;*
> *I have spread my dreams under your feet;*
> *Tread softly because you tread on my dreams.*

IT SOUNDED LIKE an earthquake.

The angel folded up his giant wings and disappeared as Joseph bolted up from bed.

More crashes and screams rose up from below. He threw on some dry clothes and ran down the stairs. His legs felt weak. The front door was wide open, and he shivered. Bags of garbage and scraps of food were spilled across the hallway, amid a trail of melting snow.

Joseph heard Albert yell, "Stop! No!" from the dining room, and he thought someone had broken into the house.

Then he heard the barking.

Madge screeched and darted past him, straight up the stairs. Joseph poked his head into the dining room, where Albert was running in circles, chasing Frankie's little white stray. The wet dog skidded around a chair and knocked it over with a crash. In the corner, the invisible bird sounded as if it was helplessly throwing itself against the walls of its cage.

Joseph joined the chase and tried to intercept the straggly dog as he leapt up onto the sideboard, scattering piles of old candles and oyster shells. Albert stretched out his arms to strangle the dripping animal, slipped on the water, and fell backwards. The dog jumped over him, like a tiny hurdler at the Olympics, but he went too fast and slid directly into the wall, smacking his head against the wainscoting. Joseph ran over, scooped him up, and marched to the front door, where Frankie stood silently, watching everything with his mouth wide open.

Joseph shoved the dog into his arms. "Get out of here," he whispered, and slammed the door in his face.

Joseph returned to the dining room and helped his uncle stand up.

"Thank you, Joseph."

"What happened?"

"That . . . *thing* snuck in when I went to take out the rubbish. Look what it did to my house!" Albert seemed on the verge of crying, or killing someone.

"I'll help clean up," said Joseph.

"No!" Albert said sharply. "Just . . . sit down here, by the fire."

He left the room and returned with a blanket, which he wrapped around Joseph. "Just sit, and keep quiet."

The clock in the hallway chimed.

Joseph was sure he heard voices in other rooms again

and footsteps above him, and then the sound of bells returned.

"Uncle Albert, what are those sounds?"

"It's nothing, Joseph."

"Is there a television somewhere around here?"

"Ha. No." There was a pause, then Joseph heard his uncle whisper, *"'Be not afeard; the isle is full of noises, sounds, and sweet airs, that give delight and hurt not.'"*

"What?"

Albert didn't answer. He just rolled up his sleeves and set to work. There was a tattoo on his forearm, the silhouette of a black ship.

"Is that the *Kraken*?" Joseph asked.

Albert seemed startled. "How do you know that name?"

"The painting of the shipwreck by the door, it says 'Kraken' on the frame. There are ships all over the place, in my room, on the roof, on *you*. Are you a sailor?"

Albert looked at his tattoo and ran his thumb across the sails.

"So you *are* a sailor."

"No, Joseph, I'm not a sailor."

"But why . . ."

His uncle drew back a curtain in the corner of the room to reveal an old Victrola. He placed a thick black record on it, hand-cranked the machine, then lowered the arm. When the needle touched the record, a crackling sound was amplified through the bright red horn. Soon the scratches gave way to a sweet, simple tune, almost like a lullaby. The music slowly grew, changed, and became more complex.

"Mozart," said Joseph.

"Yes," said Albert, surprised. "Piano Sonata in A Major."

Joseph knew the piece. Blink liked to play it on his violin.

"Your mother used to play that."

"The record?"

"No, the piece. On the piano."

Joseph had never even seen his mother listen to the radio. "My mother doesn't play the piano."

"She did," Albert said.

"Really? Why did she stop?"

Albert shrugged, but Joseph could sense a world of things his uncle wasn't saying.

As the record played, Albert picked up chairs, collected oyster shells, relit candles, and straightened the plates and silverware. When Joseph leaned over to pick up one of the broken plates, his uncle said sharply, "Joseph, stop!"

Albert lit his pipe, clamped it between his teeth, and proceeded to move all the chairs into the exact spots he wanted. He cleared the dining table, then knelt down and polished it until the table sparkled. Joseph couldn't help noticing how careful his uncle was with the surface, how he caressed it and stared at it, as if the table were the most important thing in the world.

Afterwards, Albert picked up the pieces of the shattered crystal goblets and replaced them with others from a cabinet. He arranged the food, leaving half-eaten bits on the plates, poured wine to different levels in all the glasses, and finally, with great precision, returned the napkin to the floor beneath the chair.

"What are you doing?" asked Joseph.

"Cleaning up."

"Then why are you putting the napkin back on the floor? Why did you put food on the plates? Why aren't the chairs pushed in?"

Albert ignored the questions and tended to the fire.

"But it looks exactly like it did the other night, when I saw it through the window."

Albert walked to the fireplace and carefully polished a silver object beneath the antique painting of the man with red hair.

Joseph coughed. "Who is that?"

Albert didn't even glance up at the painting. "No one."

"Is he related to us?"

"Joseph!"

"He has red hair, like us, and like Leo in the photo. Or is that Leo grown up?"

Albert squinted at Joseph in a manner that made it clear Joseph should be quiet. Then he placed the silver object back down on the mantel. The object had a lid and gold handles.

Joseph couldn't help himself. "Is that a trophy?"

"My god. I'm beginning to understand why your parents send you to boarding school. Don't you ever shut up? I'm going to make some tea and get you more of the medicine Frankie's mother brought. It seems to be helping. When I'm done I'll deliver it to you in bed. Can you make it up the stairs by yourself?"

"What's going to happen to me?" Joseph asked. "When are my parents coming back from their trip?"

"Not soon enough," Albert said under his breath as he left the room.

The thought of explaining the past few days to his parents terrified Joseph, and he tried not to think about the trouble he was in. As he stood to go upstairs, he noticed the word BELOVED engraved on a brass plaque on the marble base of the trophy. It couldn't hurt to take a quick look, he thought, so he stood on his tiptoes and lifted the lid.

The trophy was filled with some kind of grey dust that looked like ashes from the fireplace. He became distracted wondering why his uncle would save ashes, and the lid slipped from his hand, crashing to the floor. Albert was in the room in an instant.

"What are you doing?" He stormed towards Joseph, who stumbled backwards getting out of his uncle's way. The invisible bird shrieked as if in response.

"I'm sorry!" said Joseph. "I was just looking in the trophy."

Albert picked up the lid and put it back on. "It's not a trophy!"

"What is it?"

"You really want to know?"

Albert moved towards him, backing him up against the wall. "It's an *urn*."

"What's that?"

Albert let out an exasperated sigh. "When someone is cremated after they die, their ashes are put in an urn."

"Oh. I didn't know." Joseph pointed to the portrait above the fireplace. "Are they *his* ashes?"

Albert retreated to a chair and sank into it. The music

from the Victrola came to an end. The needle scratched and hissed in an endless loop, but Albert didn't move.

Something shifted on the other side of the window, and Joseph turned to see Frankie standing outside in the snow, clutching the dog, watching everything through the glass. Frankie seemed shaken by being caught and the dog leapt out of his arms. They ran off down the street.

When Joseph turned back to the dining room, his uncle had vanished, like a magic trick.

"UNCLE ALBERT? Where'd you go?"

Joseph stepped out into the hallway. He heard a noise behind the staircase, where he spotted another doorway leading down to the cellar. Joseph found his uncle in an ancient kitchen, tossing a few pieces of charcoal into an iron stove. The light through the windows had a smoky haze to it, giving the entire room a soft edge that reminded Joseph of a painting. The ceiling was low and lined with dark wooden beams. A giant hutch held rows of blue-and-white china dishes. Strange brass implements hung on either side of the stove. Cut-paper snowflakes were suspended from a narrow mantel above the fireplace, which was covered with candlesticks and knickknacks and silver jars.

The wide boards of the old floor groaned as Joseph entered. Albert wiped his hands on his apron and proceeded to make toast and tea, which they ate in silence at the cluttered table.

When he was finished, Albert walked to the far end of the table, where he pulled a fresh stalk of celery from a ceramic bowl that also held lettuce, cauliflower, carrots, and red peppers. He began to cut the celery on an old chopping board. Joseph had no idea what to do. "Can I help?"

"No."

"Why not?"

"You're still sick."

"I feel better. I want to do something."

Without looking up, Albert threw a stalk of celery in Joseph's direction. Joseph had always hated any sport that involved catching things, and the stalk bounced off his chest and hit the floor before he'd even lifted his arms.

"Your reflexes are terrible."

"What?"

"If you break anything, you're going to be sorry. Understand?"

"Um . . . no."

"You do know how to clean dishes, don't you?"

Joseph *didn't* know, actually. There had always been staff to clean up after meals, both at school and at his parents' homes.

"The apron is on the chair."

Joseph picked up one of the dirty dishes on the table, but his uncle stopped him.

"Not those." He pointed to the wall of blue-and-white porcelain behind Joseph.

"But . . . they're clean, aren't they?"

"Joseph, please . . . the apron."

So after some instruction, Joseph put on the apron and started carefully polishing the clean dishes even though it made no sense to him.

Over the course of the day, he learned how to wash the floors and clean the windows and empty out the iron stove. Soon the kitchen smelled of lemons and spices, fresh bread and soap.

There was a short break for lunch before resuming work. The light shifted during the afternoon and cascaded through the clean windows, burnishing the room with gold.

Joseph was so focused on the work, on the patterns of the silverware and the curve of the handles on the ancient pitchers and measuring cups, that he forgot for a little while about his parents, and St. Anthony's, and the fire, and losing Blink. He felt a kind of pride in being allowed to touch all the delicate glassware, plates, and bowls, and he hadn't broken a single thing.

By early evening, Joseph was sweaty and tired and his hands ached. Albert prepared them a quick dinner. After they'd eaten, he took off the apron, so Joseph took off his, too. Without another word, Albert left the room.

Joseph felt like he was waking from a daydream as he followed. "Uncle Albert! Where are you going?"

Albert continued upstairs to the ground floor, pulled out a chair at the dining room table, and sat down. "It's been a long day, Joseph. Go up to your room and rest."

Albert covered his eyes with his hands, and Joseph could tell his uncle had shut himself off and wasn't going to say anything else.

Disappointed, Joseph slowly climbed the stairs, ducking beneath the tattered laundry that hung across the landing, as if it had been put out to dry a century ago and forgotten. He imagined that a curse had been put on his uncle, condemning him to live in this house forever. Maybe Albert Nightingale was like a vampire in a novel, doomed to witness centuries going by. Maybe he was forced to work day and night to keep the future from seeping into the house, making a kind of refuge of the past, the only world he knew.

Joseph shuddered as he pushed open the green door and prepared himself for bed.

IN THE MIDDLE of the night, the ghost returned.

Or at least, Joseph thought it did. He was awakened by sounds he was sure were coming from the attic. The rest of the house was quiet, so he slipped a blanket around his shoulders, put on his shoes, lit a candle, and went to investigate. Heart pounding, he quietly climbed the crowded ladder and opened the attic door.

"Hello?" he whispered.

There was no answer.

He entered and found himself beneath old wooden beams that created a long triangular space. A small window looked out onto the roof, where blue moonlight bounced off the snow. Inside, the gold light from the candle illuminated old furniture, boxes, wrought iron signs, and empty trunks marked for Christmas. Other crates held British flags and pictures of the Queen. In the back, beneath the farthest eave, Joseph found three cartons marked simply with the letter B. They were filled with men's clothing, some covered in dirt and mud, all carefully folded. Another box, with the letters MMB, held old tools and some yellowing newspapers.

It was cold. Joseph noticed that the lock on the window was broken and the frame had warped so the window couldn't shut completely. He looked out onto the roof. Soft indentations in the snow stretched from the attic window over a small incline between four cracked red clay chimneys. A crazy thought entered Joseph's mind: What if, by some miracle, Blink had remembered his uncle's address and had made his way here, too? What if the footprints on the roof were Blink's?

Joseph pulled open the window and stepped outside. The air was freezing and the wind blew out his candle. He pulled the blanket tighter around himself. "Blink?" he whispered.

Shivering, he turned around and looked up. The golden ship that had led him here was swivelling in the wind. Joseph had never been this close to a weather vane, and he was surprised by how large it was.

He followed the footprints as far as he could, but after he'd gone over the incline, they disappeared.

The buildings were connected for the entire length of the street, and Joseph walked until he came to another attic window, lit from within. In a small room with white curtains, a girl with long black hair climbed into bed with a book. Her room looked cosy and warm, and Joseph wondered if her parents were awake downstairs, reading side by side in their bedroom or preparing tomorrow's lunch for her. The girl switched on a lamp and turned towards the window. Joseph quickly crouched down.

He didn't think she'd seen him, but his heart raced as he ran back to his uncle's house and returned to his room.

He tried to warm up under the covers with Blink's book.

Had I the heavens' embroidered cloths,
Enwrought with golden and silver light,
The blue and the dim and the dark cloths
Of night and light and the half light . . .

Joseph tried to concentrate but couldn't keep his eyes open. The book slipped to the floor and the world went up in flames.

ALBERT WAS STILL sitting in the dining room when Joseph came downstairs in the morning. His chin rested on his hand, as if he was posing for a photograph, and his eyes were red. He looked like he'd been crying.

"Were you sitting there all night?"

Albert closed his eyes.

"The fire's gone out," said Joseph.

Albert didn't move, so Joseph placed some logs on the andirons and crumpled newspaper beneath them.

"Is this okay?" asked Joseph. "I know how to make a fire."

Albert opened his eyes, looked at Joseph kneeling on the floor, and raised an eyebrow.

"Where are the matches?"

Albert slowly reached into his pocket, but his box of matches was empty. He pointed to a sideboard filled with drawers in the corner of the room. "In the silver case," he said. "On top."

Amid piles of oyster shells and several brass candlesticks, Joseph found the case. Engraved on the lid were the words *Aut Visum Aut Non*.

"What does this say?" Joseph asked.

"You learned no Latin in school?"

Joseph tried to translate. *"Search or not?"*

"Visum, not *vitum."*

"Right. Uh. *See or not?"*

"Your Latin is terrible, Joseph."

"I know."

Albert sighed. *"You either see it or you don't."*

"What does that mean?"

"It means you either see it or you don't."

"See *what?"*

"Just light the fire, Joseph. Carefully."

Soon, Joseph had a beautiful fire roaring in the fireplace. The heat and the warm orange light always brought Joseph back to the memory of his grandfather's house, and it filled him with happiness. He let the feeling soak in for a few moments before taking the matches and lighting each of the candles around the room. The words from the silver case kept running through his mind . . . *"You either see it or you don't."*

Joseph waited for his uncle to tell him to stop lighting candles, but Albert just stuffed his pipe with tobacco and said, "Bring me a match."

Joseph watched him swirl the match along the top of the tobacco and light his pipe.

The ghost bird twittered and the clock ticked.

"Is there a bird somewhere around here? I keep hearing one."

Albert rubbed his beard and wiped his eyes, then got up and left the room.

Joseph was getting used to his uncle disappearing without a word. He moved closer to the fire and stared up at the man in the painting above the fireplace. *Who are you?* thought Joseph. *What was your name?*

Just then, Joseph noticed a small plaque at the top of the gold frame. He had to squint to see it. Carved into the metal plate, barely legible, were the words *Aut Visum Aut Non.*

Albert called to him from elsewhere in the house. Joseph slipped some of the matches into his pocket and went to find his uncle.

"ARE YOU LISTENING carefully, Joseph?" Albert was lighting candles on the Christmas tree in the back parlour, talking to Joseph without looking at him. "Go down to the kitchen. Boil some water and bring the kettle upstairs. Can you do that?"

Joseph nodded and ran down to the kitchen. The kettle was heavy, but he managed to fill it with water from the sink and bring it to the stove. While he waited, Joseph poked around, opening drawers and cabinets. He discovered a small blue-and-white ceramic box hidden in the corner behind some jars of sugar and salt. The words *Aut Visum Aut Non* were painted across the lid.

"You either see it or you don't."

The words were beginning to feel like a threat. What was he not seeing?

Once the water in the kettle boiled, Joseph lugged it upstairs, using a towel he found by the sink so the hot metal handle wouldn't burn him.

Albert was cleaning out the teacups on the table in front of the sofa and laying tea strainers across the tops.

He instructed Joseph to pour the hot water over the strainers. "I don't want any," said Joseph.

"It's not for you."

"Who's it for? Is someone coming over?"

Albert laid two newly polished spoons by the teacups and walked upstairs. "Bring the kettle," he called back. Joseph followed along like a puppy, trying to keep up.

Albert entered a bedroom where ornate brocade fabrics hung from the ceiling above the bed. The fireplace in this room had been painted a beautiful bright turquoise. But even more dazzling to Joseph were the dozens of small blue-and-white Chinese vases and porcelain figures, each one sitting on its own little gold shelf, that covered the wall above the fireplace.

A half-eaten scone sat on a plate on the nightstand, and a gentleman's cane leaned against the wall. A suit hung over the back of a chair, and laundry was piled up near the bed. Albert picked up the scone and ate it. Then he reached into a pocket on his apron and removed another one, from which he took a single bite, and set it down on the table.

"Whose room is this?"

"It's mine, Joseph."

Joseph struggled with the heavy kettle. "What should I do with this?"

"Pour some water in the teacup by the fireplace, then you can put the kettle down on the hearth."

Joseph did as instructed. He watched his uncle for a few moments, then said, "What's that smell? I like it."

Albert pointed to the top of an oak dresser. An orange, completely pierced with small star-shaped objects, sat on a bed of pine needles in a ceramic dish. "It's a pomander ball," said Albert. "Orange and cloves. We make one every Christmas."

"Who's *we*?"

"I mean, *I* make one every Christmas. Now straighten the shoes in the corner."

"Do you want me to make the bed?"

"No."

The shoes in the corner were all old-fashioned black or brown leather, except for one pair made from canvas and covered in dried mud. Joseph started to brush off the mud, but Albert yelled, "Joseph, what are you doing? Stop!"

Startled, Joseph put down the shoes.

Albert opened a small closet door and took out a bin and brush. "Clean out the hearth, and don't get ashes everywhere."

On his hands and knees, Joseph felt like Cinderella. He noticed that the interior of the turquoise fireplace was lined with old sooty ceramic tiles, each about the size of his hand. All the tiles had similar blue borders with little designs painted in the centre. Some tiles had windmills and tulips, others had ships and fish, and one had two figures standing side by side, holding hands.

Albert appeared behind Joseph with a pail full of water and some rags. "Wipe down the tiles. It's been a while." He picked up the kettle. "When you're done, meet me upstairs in the sitting room."

THROUGH AN IMPOSING blue door, Joseph entered
the lady's sitting room. Albert was adjusting various
items on a lace-covered table, including a china teapot, a
delicate teacup, a pair of green earrings, and a fan. A
large portrait of a woman posing beneath curtains in a
theatre hung above a white fireplace.

Albert handed Joseph another cloth. He pointed to a
candelabra on the windowsill behind a large wingback
chair. Joseph was polishing the silver when his eye fell
on a leather-bound book on the seat of the chair. Making
sure his uncle's back was to him, he opened it. The smell
was musty and old. The title page said, *The Compleat
Works of William Shakespeare.*

There was an engraving of Shakespeare himself on the
title page, and on the opposite page, in faded brown ink,
someone had written, *This book belongs to Mabel Hatch.*

"Who is Mabel Hatch?" Joseph asked without
thinking. He pointed to the painting. "Is it her?"

Albert turned sharply. "Shut the book, Joseph.
You're only to touch what I tell you to touch."

Joseph looked again at the elegant woman in the

painting above the fireplace. She did not look like someone named Mabel Hatch. What if she was the former owner of the house, or maybe she was married to the man in the painting downstairs? Were they Leo's parents? Could Leo's last name have been Hatch?

Joseph continued to polish the candelabra as Albert organized papers on a desk.

They worked in silence for a long time.

"What's his name?" Albert's voice startled Joseph, and he looked up.

"Who?"

"Your friend. The one you told me about."

"Blink?"

"I mean, what's his *real* name?"

Joseph had never once called Blink by his real name. It felt strange to say it out loud. "George Patel."

"He's Indian?"

"Half. His mother was Greek, I think."

"Do you know his parents' names?"

"He only has a father now, a scientist. I don't know his name. Mr. Patel, maybe? Dr. Patel?"

Joseph tried to remember all the facts he could about Blink's life, but neither of them had liked talking about their families very much. "His mother left when Blink was small. His father has worked at some hospitals in

London. Blink mentioned him doing research some-where famous. I think he said his Indian grandparents pay for boarding school. They own a shop, but I don't know what kind, or even if it's in London."

"His father left no forwarding address?"

Joseph shook his head.

"So how exactly were you planning to track down this boy?"

"I don't know, I was hoping you might . . ."

"Might what?"

Joseph exhaled, as if he'd been holding his breath for too long. Maybe he'd always known it would be impossible to find Blink. He'd been a fool. A coward and a fool who believed his own made-up stories. Maybe his parents had been right. Maybe stories only led you in the wrong direction.

"Go and wash your face." Albert had to repeat himself twice before Joseph heard.

He went down to the hidden bathroom in the cellar and turned on the tap. The water was cold and it felt good, and the tears soon stopped. Joseph cleaned his glasses and looked into the mirror at his red eyes, his messy hair, and his rumpled shirt. He almost didn't recognize the boy who stared back at him from the other side of the glass. He realized there was nothing to do but go back to work.

JOSEPH WAS READING in bed when the clock
struck six. The door to his bedroom opened and Albert
appeared, wearing a faded black tuxedo and shiny
black shoes. His red hair was slicked down and parted
on the side. He delivered supper on a tray to the
nightstand.

"Can I trust you alone in this house?" Albert asked
Joseph.

"What? Yes. Why?"

"I need to go out for the evening. And the house can
never be left unattended while any fires are burning,
and I mean candles as well as the fireplace here in your
room."

"Where are you going?"

"Do you promise not to let my house burn down?"

"Can I come with you?"

"Joseph, answer my question."

"Yes," said Joseph. "I promise."

"You have your books. Supper is hot. Just assure me
you'll stay in bed and read when you finish eating."

"Right, but—"

"No buts. Just eat dinner and read. You're still recovering and shouldn't go outside yet."

"Alright."

Albert turned and went downstairs. Where in the world was his uncle going?

Joseph's curiosity got the better of him, so he bolted from his bed and tiptoed out of his room. He watched unseen from the stairwell as his uncle moved from room to room, extinguishing the candles and the fires. Then Albert put on his long fur coat and his hat and left the house.

Joseph snuck into the dining room and peered through the window. To his astonishment, he saw a nineteenth-century horse-drawn carriage, as if it had been conjured by the house itself from the mysterious sounds Joseph had been hearing. The horse was dark and shiny, outfitted with black leather and an assortment of brass fittings and worn ropes. A man wearing a checked wool coat, a long scarf, and a leather top hat helped Albert into the carriage. Joseph recognized him immediately as the French fishmonger from the market. He climbed up to a seat on the roof, raised his whip, and they trotted off. In a minute, the carriage disappeared down the street, followed by the little white dog, which seemed to have appeared from nowhere.

Joseph walked through the dim shadows of the dining room, careful not to move a chair or dislodge a napkin. The distant voices and faraway footsteps he kept hearing echoed through the chamber, like the voices of ghosts trapped in the walls. Joseph shivered and lit a candle.

He now had free rein to explore the house.

Following the circle of dim gold light cast by the candle, he went up the stairs and, feeling like a prowler, he poked his head into Albert's bedroom. Joseph didn't know what he was looking for exactly. But the house felt like a puzzle, and maybe if he put together the pieces, he could *solve* it. Without Blink, or any hope of seeing him again, all Joseph had left, it seemed, was this mysterious house and its links to the distant past and to a boy he might be related to named Leo.

Everything in his uncle's room was just as he'd left it earlier, except his apron was hanging on a hook by the fireplace. The half-eaten scone still sat on the plate; the shoes, including the muddy ones, were still lined up neatly; and the tiles in the turquoise fireplace gleamed.

One flight up, Joseph pushed open the blue door and explored the lady's sitting room. The candlelight illuminated the cup of tea and the teapot on the lace-covered table, as well as the pair of green earrings, and the fan his uncle had adjusted so carefully.

Joseph stared up into the eyes of the woman in the painting, and he thought for a moment she had an expression like his own mother's, a look he didn't know quite how to describe, except that it seemed as if the rest of the world was being judged.

As he gazed at the painting, he realized with a shiver that the woman was wearing green earrings and held a fan in her right hand—almost exactly like the earrings and the fan on the table. Suddenly, it felt as if the woman was alive and had just set down her things before stepping out of the room. Joseph half expected her to walk back in at any moment.

You either see it or you don't, he thought. What was it? What was he missing?

He looked around. Perhaps this room held the key to all his uncle's secrets.

Joseph set down the candle and opened the Shakespeare book with great care.

This book belongs to Mabel Hatch.

He flipped through it, stopping randomly to read a line or two from the plays:

"The moon's an arrant thief, And her pale fire she snatches from the sun . . ."

"A sad tale's best for winter . . ."

"The iron tongue of midnight hath told twelve.

Lovers, to bed; 'tis almost faerie time . . ."

Church bells rang, and the air in the room seemed to swell.

Please, Joseph thought. *Help me! Someone help me!*

At that exact moment, as if kindled by Joseph's thoughts, two ghostly fingers formed out of the dusty air and tapped him twice on the shoulder.

He screamed and spun around.

Standing in the dim light was *Frankie,* in his blue cap, smiling like the Cheshire Cat.

"You scared me!" hissed Joseph. "How did you get in? Uncle Albert will kill *both* of us if he finds you here!"

"We're safe for a while," said Frankie. "He's at the theatre. He doesn't come back till late."

"How do you know that?"

"I followed his carriage a couple of times on my bike."

"Frankie! Are you mad? Get out of here!"

"No!"

Frankie didn't budge, so Joseph put his hands on the boy's shoulders and tried to force him towards the door. Frankie pushed back, and suddenly the two of them were wrestling on the floor. Joseph accidentally kicked the table, sending the green earrings and everything else clattering across the room. The delicate china teacup shattered and tea spilled all over the carpet. The handle snapped off the teapot. Silverware scattered.

Joseph shrieked in horror, and in his desperate struggle to stand up, he pulled off Frankie's cap. A wave of long black hair came tumbling down.

Joseph stumbled backwards. "You're . . . a *girl*?"

FRANKIE GRABBED HER cap back from Joseph, who flushed with embarrassment. This was the same girl he'd spied in her room across the roof the other night. It must have been *her* footprints he'd seen in the snow.

"You didn't know I was a girl?"

"Yes! No! I mean . . . your name is *Frankie*! That's a boy's name!"

"It's short for *Frances*," she said, panting, "which is a girl's name." Frankie tucked her hair back up into her cap. "Well, good. I don't mind if you thought I was a boy."

Joseph looked down at the damage on the carpet. "Oh god! You need to get out of here. I've got to clean this up."

"I'll help."

"No! Don't touch anything!" Joseph glared at Frankie, aware of how much he sounded like his uncle. "Do you always break into people's houses?"

"Just this one."

"But that's illegal, Frankie! It's *trespassing*! Why would you do that?"

They heard a noise behind them and jumped, thinking Albert had returned early. But it was just Madge, sidling against the door. Joseph surveyed the damage and was so upset his hands shook. He knew that any progress he might have made with his uncle, any trust he might have earned, had shattered along with the teacup.

Joseph turned the table and chairs upright and located one of the earrings and the fan. He hoped the tea wouldn't stain too badly. He spotted some of the silverware shining in a corner.

"I'm going to help," said Frankie. "You can't stop me."

Joseph glared at her. "Fine . . . just find the other earring."

Frankie and Joseph scoured the floor, sweeping their hands across the carpet. Joseph began to reassemble everything on the tabletop as best he could remember.

"Joseph," said Frankie.

"What?"

"Can I ask you something?"

"No."

Frankie ignored him. "Is your uncle sick?"

This was the last thing he thought she was going to say. "*Sick?* He's not sick. Why would you ask me something like that?"

"I mean, I've seen him go into my mum's clinic, and she treats people who are *dying*. Sometimes people even think my mum is sick just because she works there, but she told me she's safe and you can't get it just from touching someone."

"Get *what*?"

"AIDS. Princess Diana even came last year for a visit to show people you can't catch it just from being near someone. My mum met her."

Was his uncle really *dying*? He didn't look like he was dying, but Joseph had never known anyone who was that sick. Even his grandfather had looked healthy when he'd visited him in California a few months before he died. At least that's how he remembered it.

"Uncle Albert is not dying," said Joseph, as if it was a fact.

Frankie was quiet for a moment, and then asked, "Why'd you do it?"

"Do *what*?"

"Run away. I saw your suitcase. Were you getting beaten at school?"

"What? *No!*"

"In films and books, children are always getting beaten at school, and then they run away."

"That's not why I ran away."

"Well, you must be a brave person. I couldn't do it."

The words surprised Joseph. He'd been a *coward* at school when Blink wanted him to run away in October. But now that he was in London on his own, maybe it meant he *was* brave.

"Can I tell you something?" Frankie asked as they continued to clean the room.

"Frankie. Please don't."

"I think Marcus might be connected to your uncle somehow, and to the house."

"Marcus? You mean *the dog*?"

"No! My *brother*."

"You have a brother?"

"I did. Marcus Matthew Bloom."

Joseph set down the spoons and forks on the table. "But . . . what happened to him?"

"I'm not sure exactly. I think it was an accident. I was only five when he died. I don't remember much. He was a lot older. My parents never talk about him. My mum's knackered when she comes home from the clinic, and my dad only really likes to talk about baking, and birds."

"Birds?"

"He's a bird-watcher. He goes to Victoria Park with his binoculars whenever he can." She adjusted the cap on her head. "Anyway, I remember Marcus was nice to me. He used to give me things he found by the river, little treasures he told me had washed up on the shore. I always loved them. I still have them." Frankie looked down at her feet. "I feel like I must be a disappointment to my parents, especially my mum. I imagine she wishes I was more like *him*. But I know her job is hard, and I try not to worry her."

"Well, maybe you should stop breaking into people's houses."

"What would *you* do? I like to play on the roof and I can see right into your uncle's attic. One afternoon I was looking inside . . . and I saw a box with the letters MMB written on it. My *brother's initials*. Could *you* ignore that?"

Joseph had seen the box, which was mostly empty except for some old tools and newspapers. "Maybe it was just a coincidence."

"Maybe. But the window was open, so I climbed in, and inside the box were all these glass jars . . ."

"There were? I didn't see any glass jars."

"That's because I took them."

"Frankie! You shouldn't be pinching things from my uncle!"

"I know. But maybe they belonged to Marcus."

"Why?"

"They were filled with all the same kinds of treasures he used to give me from the river. Pieces of china, bits of clay or stone, rusty nails. Old things. Maybe he was going to give them to me." Frankie, still on her hands and knees, said, "Oh! What's this?" She held up a small key tied with a frayed blue ribbon.

"That must go on the table, too," said Joseph. "I didn't see it before. Put it near the fan."

"Don't you want to know what it opens?"

"No, Frankie!" said Joseph, even though he wanted very much to know. He just didn't want Frankie around when he found out. "I'm in enough trouble already. And so are you. Just find the other earring."

Joseph and Frankie searched in silence for a while. Madge edged closer to them, as if she wanted to supervise their progress. Finally, Joseph spotted the other earring, sparkling at the edge of the fireplace. "I found it!"

He stood and turned to see Frankie slipping the key into a cabinet in the desk.

"Me, too," she said.

"Frankie! Leave it alone."

"I know you're curious." She opened the cabinet and reached inside. She pulled out an old shoe box tied with yellowing strings. Handwritten across the top of the box were the words *Aut Visum Aut Non.*

"What does that mean?" asked Frankie.

"I don't know," Joseph lied.

"Well, open it."

"No. Put it back."

"I'll do it, then." She grabbed for the box.

"No, stop. I'll do it." Joseph picked at the knots until they loosened, then gently lifted the lid. The shoe box was filled with stacks of cassette tapes, each in its own clear plastic case.

"What do you think is on them?" asked Frankie.

"I don't know. Music, maybe?"

"Do you have a cassette player?"

"No."

"My mum does. Shall I take them?"

"No! We can't steal anything else."

Joseph put the lid back on the box, returned it to the cabinet, and locked the little door. He'd figure out how to listen to them later, on his own. It was his puzzle to solve, anyway. He put the key beneath the fan on the table.

From across the room, Frankie said, "Oberon and Eleanora Marvel."

"What? *Who?*"

Frankie was standing at the desk, holding an envelope in her hand, reading. "*'Oberon and Eleanora Marvel,'*" she repeated, then looked at Joseph as she gave the envelope to him. "Who are they?" she asked. "Their names are on this."

The envelope was light and brittle in Joseph's hand.

Oberon and Eleanora Marvel
18 Folgate Street
London

"They must have lived here," said Frankie. "Don't you think?" She then pointed to the painting of the woman on the wall. "Do you think *that* could be Eleanora Marvel?"

"Oh, maybe! Yes," said Joseph, liking the idea very much. The name Eleanora Marvel seemed to make more sense for this beautiful woman. It was a much better name than Mabel Hatch, anyway. And maybe that meant the man in the painting downstairs was Oberon Marvel. But who was Mabel Hatch, then?

"Wait here for a second!" Joseph ran up the stairs to his room and retrieved the flower-embossed leather case. He raced back down, opened it, and handed it to Frankie.

"This is Leo. It's a black-and-white photograph of him, but see how someone coloured his hair *red*? Maybe he was Oberon and Eleanora's *son*. That would make his name Leo *Marvel*!"

"Do you think he drew that angel?" asked Frankie.

"I guess so."

"He is a good artist. *Was* a good artist."

Joseph agreed.

"So this was their house. The *Marvels*."

"That must be it. Right?"

"Did your parents ever talk about ancestors in London?"

Joseph looked up from the photograph. "That's what's confusing me. My mother and my uncle are *American*," Joseph said. "They're from California. So why would *their* ancestors be here in London? It's my *father's* side that's English. My mother didn't come here until she got married. But the Jervis side are all bankers and barristers from Surrey, and none of them has red hair, as far as I know."

"Maybe they still live here," said Frankie. "The Marvels, I mean. They're still here, like ghosts! Maybe that's why your uncle keeps the house like this."

"There's no such things as ghosts, Frankie. But . . ."

"But what?"

"Well, sometimes I hear voices in other rooms, and footsteps, and a bird . . ."

"A bird?"

"Like a canary or something. And the first night I was

here, I had a fever, and I thought I saw Leo's ghost."

Frankie's cheeks turned bright red. "Oh, Joseph, didn't you realize?"

"What?"

"That was *me*. I snuck in, to find out what was going on, but when I opened your door, you screamed and I ran back to the attic . . . but that doesn't mean the house isn't *really* haunted."

Joseph, overwhelmed by everything, slipped the leather case with the photograph into his pocket and said, "Frankie, you should go now. My uncle might be back soon."

Ignoring him, Frankie reached over and picked up another piece of paper from the desk. It was an old theatre programme, creased and torn around the edges. She and Joseph read it together.

THE TEMPEST
A Play by William Shakespeare
Starring Oberon and Eleanora Marvel
At the Royal Theatre
13 January 1900

"Look!" said Frankie. "They're actors! And it says they performed at the *Royal Theatre*. That's the theatre your uncle goes to all the time. That's where he is right now! Do you think he's an actor, too, like the Marvels?"

Joseph almost laughed. "If you spent any time with him, you wouldn't ask that question."

"Well, I guess we'd better go for a visit, then."

Joseph looked at Frankie like she was mad. "A visit *where*?"

"To the theatre! Maybe we can find out what's going on! There has to be a connection between the theatre and your uncle and the Marvels, right? And maybe with Marcus, too."

"I can't leave the house. I promised him I'd stay in my room."

"You've obviously broken that promise already. We'll make sure he doesn't find out!"

Joseph hesitated. "We can't do this, Frankie."

"It's too late to be scared, Joseph. Don't you want to understand what's going on?"

Joseph stared at Frankie. She was right.

"I just have one question for you," she said.

"What?"

"Where's your winter coat?"

IT TOOK A WHILE for them to get to the theatre with Joseph riding on the handlebars of Frankie's bike. It was cold, but Joseph barely noticed because he was so nervous and the bike was bumping so wildly. When they arrived, Frankie locked her bike to a street sign. A huge banner hung between the centre columns of the theatre: THE WINTER'S TALE BY WILLIAM SHAKESPEARE.

The world is filled with Shakespeare, thought Joseph.

Across from the theatre they spotted Albert's horse and carriage tied to a metal post in front of a pub, where the driver with the leather top hat sat inside at a table by the window. The show had already begun, and the grand front doors of the theatre were locked.

"There has to be another way in," said Frankie. She motioned for Joseph to follow her, and they made their way to the back of the building, where a sign read STAGE DOOR.

They peeked through the glass panels in the doors. Inside was a narrow hallway and a cramped office, where an old man with his back to them was smoking a cigarette. He faced a small black-and-white TV monitor.

"What do we do?" whispered Frankie. "There's a guard!"

"I knew this was a bad idea . . ."

Frankie reached for the latch. It clicked and opened. She smiled. "That was *much* easier than I thought it was going to be! Come on!"

The narrow hallway was lit by an ancient light fixture and filled with the recent memory of cigarette smoke. Joseph and Frankie slipped past the guard and followed a well-worn royal blue carpet through a door, down another hallway, and up an ancient cast-iron spiral staircase.

The cracked yellow walls were lined with electric lights in wire cages, posters for old shows, and photographs of actors who had appeared in the theatre over the years. Joseph kept his eye out for Oberon and Eleanora Marvel, and even scanned quickly for any pictures of his uncle. At the top of the stairs, they continued through another door, turned a corner, and found themselves backstage.

The play was in progress. Actors and crew were scurrying about, getting ready for their scenes and putting scenery into place. From the back, everything seemed to be built out of plywood and canvas. It smelled dusty and alive, a strange combination of sweat and wood and candles and electricity, as if the air still contained the essence of everyone who'd ever walked through the building. Curtains, scenery, and lights were fixed to huge metal poles that hung from the rafters. Miles of rope crisscrossed the space, running up towards the ceiling, turning on pulleys, and coming down the walls, where weights and other mechanisms held the rigging in place. It was like being aboard a ship, thought Joseph.

They eventually made their way into a fancy curving hallway with mirrored walls. An old woman in a dark red suit and a name tag on her black vest sat in a folding chair, amid a pile of programmes. She had a book on her lap and was nodding off. Frankie and Joseph made sure both of her eyes were closed before taking a programme and tiptoeing past her, through a set of beautiful gilded doors. They slipped into the last row of seats at the back of the theatre and sat down. Thankfully, no one seemed to notice.

Joseph looked below into the cavernous space. Hundreds of people sat in red velvet seats and in gold filigreed balconies. The stage was massive, with vast red-and-gold curtains drawn back to reveal a magnificent make-believe forest with a rolling painted ocean at the back of the wooden deck.

Frankie nudged him and pointed upwards.

A huge crystal chandelier hung from the domed ceiling. Inside the dome was a painting of an angel, his great white wings spread out across a dazzling sky, as if captured midflight. The angel's head was turned, and his sweet face seemed to be watching over the audience from the clouds. In one of the angel's hands was a sword, glinting in the sunlight, and in the other hand was a lantern, burning a small flame.

"It's the angel Leo drew," whispered Frankie.

"I see it!" Joseph imagined Leo, perhaps a century ago, looking up at this same angel and drawing it on a small scrap of paper. Joseph's heart leapt at the idea that this all might be part of his family history . . . perhaps his ancestors really *had* been actors and artists! What if Joseph's cold, rich parents were the *exceptions* on his family tree, not him? Maybe every other generation, the ones he'd never known, had been full of brilliant adventurers and romantic dreamers, like himself.

Frankie interrupted his thoughts and nodded towards the stage. "Can you figure out what's going on?"

Joseph looked down at the actors and shook his head. "Maybe it says something in here." He opened the programme and found a synopsis of the play, which he and Frankie read together.

In the first act, King Leontes is living happily with his pregnant wife, Queen Hermione, and their young son, Mamillius. But then the king falsely accuses his wife of betraying him. She goes to prison and gives birth there right before she dies. Young Mamillius dies, too, although Joseph couldn't work out why *he* died. Maybe it was from grief. The newborn baby girl is abandoned in a forest.

Then, in the second act, the character of Time lets it be known that sixteen years have passed—Joseph loved how Shakespeare made all those years disappear—and the baby abandoned in the woods has grown into a beautiful young woman named Perdita. She falls in love with a prince and is eventually returned to her father, the king, who now understands how wrong he'd been all those years ago. He is shown a marble statue of his long-dead wife, and then, a miracle. The statue comes to life, and King Leontes is reunited with both his daughter and his lost queen, who has forgiven him for all the heartache and grief he'd caused their family.

Joseph turned his attention back to the stage and was quickly swept up in the action. He watched in amazement as the statue of the queen raised her arms and welcomed back her repentant husband and grown-up daughter.

The lights went up as the play ended, and Joseph

felt as if he was coming out of a trance. Frankie's face seemed to indicate she felt the same way, but the noise of the crowd quickly made Joseph panic. He had to get home before Albert did.

He grabbed Frankie's arm and ran as fast as he could through the theatre. But there were so many people, and he lost her in the rush for the doors. Outside, the cold air hit Joseph's face like a slap. He was frantically trying to find Frankie when he felt a hand on his shoulder. He spun around, but it wasn't her.

"Joseph," Albert said. The bewilderment in his voice was clear. "What are you doing here?"

"I . . . I'm sorry!"

Joseph spotted Frankie across the street, staring at him, wide-eyed. He mouthed the word "Go" and she unlocked her bike and rode off.

"Was that Frankie? What in the . . ."

The man with the leather top hat stepped forwards and opened the carriage door.

Albert glared at Joseph. "Did you extinguish all the candles before you left? Did you put out the fire in the fireplace?"

Joseph froze. How could he have let this happen again? How could he be so irresponsible? He imagined a candle falling over, the way it had on his desk, and the entire place igniting. He began to shake.

"Who is this young man, Nightingale?" asked the driver, still holding open the door.

"An untrustworthy, dangerous child," Albert said as he climbed up into the carriage. "Take me home."

"Can I ride with you?" Joseph asked.

Albert shut the door in his face.

"But I don't know how to get to the house," he yelled through the window. "It was a long ride here!"

The driver turned around and whispered to Joseph, "Climb on the back and hold on tight!" He winked. "Hurry!"

THE CARRIAGE CLATTERED along cobblestoned streets, beneath lampposts, and past statues of dragons along the edge of the river. Joseph crouched on a small platform on the back of the vehicle while struggling to keep his arm looped through a metal handle. In this uncomfortable position, he imagined returning to the house and finding it consumed by a violent column of orange flames, reaching skywards like a snapping, hissing monster. Joseph's whole body ached, and he was freezing. He couldn't stop thinking about the trouble he was in, but he also found himself haunted by *The Winter's Tale*. The play had left him strangely sad, even though he knew it was supposed to have a happy ending. Young Prince Mamillius, the king's son, had not been resurrected like the queen, or saved like the baby daughter. Time itself had appeared on stage to tell everyone that sixteen years had passed, yet the innocent young prince, like the Little Match Girl, had died for no good reason, something Joseph always hated in stories. Why couldn't there have been one more miracle for the prince?

The carriage finally turned on to the streets around

his uncle's house, and then stopped in front of 18 Folgate Street. The house sat as it always had, unconsumed by fire. Joseph let out his breath as his uncle burst from the carriage and ran straight inside the house, slamming the door behind him.

Before Joseph could jump off, the driver called back, "Hold on a moment." The carriage moved around the corner and slowed once more to a stop. Joseph lowered his legs to the ground and stretched himself out as the driver came to meet him. "Ah, good, you are alive! I worried you'd fallen off somewhere and I'd have to scrape you from the street." The man smiled, revealing the small gap between his front teeth.

"I'm alright," said Joseph. "Thank you for the lift."

"De rien," the man said in French.

"He thought I burned his house down," said Joseph.

"No, no. Of course not. He's just a worried man, Nightingale. That's all."

Joseph didn't move. He was afraid to go inside and face his uncle.

"I saw you at the market the other night, didn't I," said the man, "with Frankie?"

"Yes."

"Tell me who you are, young man."

"Joseph."

The man shook Joseph's hand firmly. "I'm Florent." He pronounced it the French way, so the T was silent. "I hear you are *untrustworthy* and *dangerous*." The Frenchman smiled. "How exciting! But I'm afraid you seem perhaps too small to be very *dangerous*, and as for *untrustworthy*, we shall see, I suppose. Tell me how you know our Nightingale."

"He's my uncle."

"Ah! Of course! I should have guessed you were related. A family of red birds, I see. You are staying with him now?"

"Yes."

"Before you go in, why don't we have a little *tête-à-tête*?"

Even though Joseph had studied French in school for many years, he wasn't sure what that meant.

Florent motioned him towards some steps and they sat. "Now . . . Nightingale never told me he had a nephew. I hope that is not insulting to you."

"We'd never met until a few days ago."

"Interesting! I've known him for a long time, since we first came to London. Him from America and me from France, could you guess?"

Joseph grinned.

"And somehow we both ended up here."

"London?"

"Specifically, *Spitalfields.*"

"Oh."

"Have you seen the Black Tulip?"

"Is it a film?"

"Well, yes, there is a film by that name, based on a book, but I meant the *pub* where I worked years ago. The Black Tulip is near Bloom's Bakery, the one Frankie's father owns."

"I've seen the bakery."

"It's not too far from there. Well, your uncle used to come in all the time, and I would spot him around town, in shops, in parks, in museums. Eventually we came to talk, *hello, hello,* and once, for a reason I cannot now remember, I told him of my childhood in Provence, the horses I rode and loved as a boy. Well! How his face lit up! He had just bought his horse and carriage, quite old, and asked would I like to work for him sometimes. Be his groomsman and driver. I always say, the more work the better, why not? Who wants to be bored? Or poor? Well, that's how I met Rachel there." He nodded towards the old horse standing patiently on the street. "Yes, our sturdy friend knows these streets by heart. Like your uncle. Nightingale could talk and talk. He knows the tiniest detail of the entire city. I learned much vocabulary from him . . . the *facade* of a building, the *mullion* of a window, the *coat of arms* on a roof. But one thing he never spoke of was family."

"My mum never really talked about *him*, either, to be fair."

"I somehow didn't picture him with a family at all. Funny, no? What did I think? Maybe I just imagined he was born fully formed, like that goddess from the head of Zeus."

"Athena," said Joseph.

"Exactly. Like her. Ah, well. We all have families, no?"

Joseph wasn't sure what to say.

"You are here for Christmas holiday from school, then?"

"Sort of."

"Well, so nice to visit your uncle and meet him finally."

"I guess so."

"The visit isn't going very well?"

"He wasn't really expecting me."

"No? It was a surprise? How did you manage that?"

"I . . . ran away."

"Ah, I had a feeling. I saw your suitcase in the market. Even more exciting!"

"No . . . he's going to kill me."

"Why would our Nightingale do that? Tell me why he is angry with you. Why are you *untrustworthy* and *dangerous*?"

"I . . . broke some things in his house, a teacup and teapot, and I didn't put out the fires before I left tonight. He doesn't like me."

"Oh, I'm sure that's not true. You seem likable enough to me." Once again he smiled. "And . . . broken things can be fixed, can't they?" There was a long silence. Finally Florent said, "Okay, maybe it's best you go inside now. Your uncle will think you are clever for finding your way back so quickly."

The two of them stood up.

"Little Nightingale, before you go, can I give you some advice?" Florent adjusted his leather top hat. "Be gentle with your uncle. He's a delicate man, like the teacup, I'm afraid."

"My *uncle*? He's not a delicate man."

"He is. He has shut himself up in that house for a long time now, and you are the first person inside in many years. Did you know that? Did you know his house used to be filled with parties and laughter? Everyone in the neighbourhood loved walking through those doors, like a voyage back in time . . ."

"Really?" Joseph couldn't imagine his uncle allowing anyone in the house, and he certainly couldn't imagine a party there. "What happened?"

"You do not know?"

"No . . ."

"Well, it is not my place to tell, then. Just be gentle. And don't be afraid of him. He's had a hard time, and is sad."

"Why?"

"Albert will tell when he's ready, I suppose." Florent turned towards the horse and ran his hand along the animal's black flank. "I must get Rachel here to her stable. She needs her sleep, as do we all, no?"

Joseph smiled.

"Remember, Little Nightingale, you can always stop doing dangerous things. And you can *prove* yourself trustworthy, right? Start by forgiving your uncle for his anger. That would be a nice gift."

Joseph had no idea what Florent was talking about, but he waved as the Frenchman climbed back up to the driver's seat and rode off with Rachel into the cold night.

JOSEPH WAS SURPRISED to find the front door unlocked. The painted shipwreck in the hallway seemed to sink beneath the black waves as he entered and locked the door behind him.

The house was terribly silent. Was it possible Albert hadn't noticed the mess? If he had gone straight to bed maybe Joseph could finish cleaning everything up.

He crept up the stairs and poked his head into Eleanora's room.

"Did you enjoy the ride back from the theatre?" Albert's voice was quiet and cold. He was sitting in a chair by the window. The shards of the teacup were at his feet. A single candle glowed by his side.

"You knew I was . . ."

"I heard Florent whispering to you, because that man whispers like he's got a megaphone. I was too tired to have you thrown off. How did you know I was at the theatre?"

"Frankie told me . . ."

"Frankie's your spy now?"

"No, that's not what I meant."

Albert carefully lit his pipe and clouds of smoke escaped from his mouth. "What have you done?"

"I'm sorry," Joseph whispered.

"You're worse than the dog. At least the dog didn't know what it did was *wrong* when it broke into my home. Go upstairs. Pack your things."

"Please! Let me explain. I'm just trying to understand what's going on around here."

"It's none of your business, Joseph."

"I have a right to know about my family!"

Albert stared at Joseph.

"I've figured it out. *Aut Visum Aut Non. You either see it or you don't.* I see it now! Oberon has red hair, like us. He was married to Eleanora . . . they performed together at the Royal Theatre, where you went tonight . . . Leo is their son. He drew the angel in the theatre. This is their *house*!"

Pipe smoke drifted in clouds around Albert's head.

"I'm right, aren't I? *Aren't I?*"

"Joseph . . ."

"But I haven't worked it *all* out."

"Good."

"Why is that good?"

"Because it's *my* house."

"But it's connected to *me*!"

"It has nothing to do with you, Joseph."

"I promise I'll fix everything! I'll have it done by tomorrow. I swear!"

"You won't be here tomorrow." Albert locked the pipe between his teeth, took the candle, and walked to the door. He turned. "In the morning, I'm calling your headmaster again. I'm going to tell him that if he doesn't take you back immediately or put me in touch with some other relative of yours, I'm going to kick you out on the street. Then *he* can explain it all to your parents when they come back from their holiday."

"Uncle Albert!"

"So listen carefully . . . if you really want to destroy my house, Joseph, I guess this will be your last chance. Go ahead. Burn everything down to the ground till there's nothing left but ash."

Albert turned and disappeared from the room, leaving only silence in his wake.

"FRANKIE! FRANKIE!"

Joseph had run across the snowy roof and was knocking frantically on her window.

She jumped up from her desk and opened it. "Joseph! What in the . . ."

"Let me in, please?"

"Hurry, it's freezing out there."

Joseph handed her his suitcase and climbed into her room.

"What do you have in here? Rocks?" Frankie closed the window behind Joseph and dropped the suitcase on the floor with a thud. "What happened? He was really angry, wasn't he?"

"He's sending me away! Can I stay here tonight? Please?"

"Yes! Of course." Frankie quickly closed the curtains. "Albert doesn't know you're gone?"

"Not yet."

Joseph lifted his suitcase onto Frankie's bed and unclasped it. Sitting on top of all his books was the white box, tied with strings.

"You took the cassettes!"

Joseph knew Florent wanted him to prove himself trustworthy to Albert, but he was desperate. Albert had written *Aut Visum Aut Non* on the box, and since there were no other clues for him to follow, he had to hear the tapes. The Latin words seemed to hint at some connection to the secrets Joseph couldn't see yet, as if the explanation was right in front of him, but the room was dark and he just needed to find the light switch. "You said your parents have a cassette player."

"My mum. My dad doesn't live here. His flat's above the bakery, remember?"

"Oh, right."

"Divorced."

"Right. Sorry. So . . . where is the cassette player?"

"In the front room."

"Can we use it now?"

"We'd wake my mum. We'll listen in the morning, after she's gone to work. Right now, though, we have to figure out where to hide you." Frankie looked around. "Luckily, my mum hardly ever comes in here." She pointed to a spot behind the door and pulled a rolled-up sleeping bag from beneath her bed.

Joseph helped to clear the floor and said, "How often do you see your dad, then?"

"On weekends I stay with him sometimes, and some holidays. I was there for Christmas. He gave me that Polaroid camera." She pointed to it on her desk. "And he always makes me a giant cake for my birthday."

"He sounds nice."

"He's alright. Not very talkative, which is why I think he likes looking at birds. You have to stay really quiet when he's bird-watching. But it's fun to be in the park with him when the weather's not too cold."

While Frankie set up the sleeping bag, Joseph noticed a grainy photograph on her nightstand. In the picture, a teenager in a black T-shirt was leaning against a brick wall. He was wearing the same blue cap Frankie always wore. "Is this Marcus?"

Frankie nodded.

Joseph studied the photo and found himself thinking about young Prince Mamillius, who died because he didn't get a miracle in *The Winter's Tale*.

"Frankie?" Joseph whispered as he climbed into the sleeping bag. "Do you know about amber?"

"*Amber?* What do you mean? The colour?"

"The stone. Have you ever seen a piece of amber with an insect stuck inside it?"

"Maybe." She got into bed and turned off the light.

"Amber starts off as sap from a tree," Joseph said in

the dark. "And sometimes insects get caught in it, and over millions of years the amber turns into a gemstone, but it traps the insect inside."

"Oh."

"A photograph is sort of like that, don't you think?"

"What do you mean?"

"It's like . . . a moment of frozen time. Marcus in the photograph is like the insect caught in amber. Frozen forever, just like that."

A long time passed and Joseph thought Frankie had fallen asleep. But then he heard her rustle in her bed, and she said something he couldn't quite hear.

"What, Frankie?"

"Sorry. I was just thinking."

"About what?"

"Running away."

"Really? I thought you said you couldn't do it," Joseph said, surprised.

"Oh, I couldn't! Mostly because my mum would have a heart attack. Especially after Marcus, well, you know. And my father wouldn't be too happy, either. But I mean, when I grow up . . . I want to go as far from London as possible. I want to go somewhere scary and exciting, like, I don't know . . . the Amazon jungle, or the pyramids in Giza!" Frankie paused. "I keep a list with all the places I want to visit, and there's a globe in my cupboard with pins stuck in it for each place. I want to see the world."

"I don't," said Joseph.

"You don't?"

"No." Joseph pulled the sleeping bag tightly around himself. "I've seen enough of it. My parents have moved from London to Saudi Arabia to Hong Kong to Germany. Everything's constantly being uprooted." He thought about Blink, and how nothing had ever felt stable to either of them except for their friendship, while it lasted.

"So what *do* you want?" asked Frankie.

"I want a *home*," said Joseph. "A proper home."

THUNDER CRACKED and the angel fell out of the sky.

For a moment, Joseph couldn't figure out where he was, but then Frankie was there, shaking him.

"Joseph, get up! My mum's at the clinic till five. We have the house to ourselves!"

Joseph jumped out of the sleeping bag, grabbed the box of cassettes, and followed Frankie down the stairs to the front room. A large stereo system sat on a shelving unit next to a boxy television set. Frankie turned it on. Joseph pulled out a cassette, slipped it into the player, and pressed play. The wheels of the cassette began to turn in tandem. He and Frankie sat on the rug and waited. At first there was only static, and then something that sounded like laughter. Joseph adjusted the volume.

"*. . . a sad woman . . .*" was the first thing they heard. *"She was brought low by a series of bad men . . ."*

Frankie clicked the stop button. "It's not music. Who is talking?"

"I'm not sure. My uncle, I guess."

"It doesn't sound like him."

"I think he's younger."

Joseph pressed play again. *". . . and soon she became pregnant . . ."*

Frankie clicked the stop button again. *"Who* became pregnant?"

"Stop pressing stop!" He hit the play button.

". . . When she gave birth, the midwife thought the baby was dead, so she placed the child in the dustbin, but a nursemaid spotted some movement, lifted the baby, and cried, 'Heavens! It's alive!'"

Joseph's eyes grew wide as he listened, and Frankie said, "Oh!"

Joseph had never heard a story like this.

"Obedience Hatch named the baby Mabel . . ."

Joseph almost jumped up. Mabel Hatch! From the Shakespeare book!

"She and her mother were terribly poor. They lived in the East End of London, and when she was old enough, Mabel worked in a factory. She despised the poverty she was trapped in.

"She was so unhappy, she'd wander home after the factory closed and stare into the fancy shop windows, dreaming of a different kind of life. But all she had were small scraps of fabric she found in the streets and old newspapers, so she made dolls from the scraps and imagined they were rich ladies. She'd make up voices for

each of them, and sometimes the other children in the factory would gather around her during their brief lunch break to listen to her as she pretended she'd come to save them with her vast wealth.

"But nothing really changed for Mabel until the day she found a book in the street. She always said it had fallen from someone's bag, although if you ask me, I think she stole it!"

Another voice on the tape said, *"What was the book?"*

"A collection of Shakespeare plays, of all things. It's the book she taught herself to read with. The language was almost impossible to understand, but she kept at it and soon came to imagine a world bigger than her own, one with magicians and fairies and kings and queens. She dreamed she was inside Shakespeare's world, inside his words, and she found herself desperate to grow up and escape her miserable life. She wanted to be a queen!

"Of course, Mabel Hatch was lucky because she had three things that were helpful to a poor woman at the time . . . she was beautiful, she was smart, and she could read. So one night, when she was a little older, working for some extra money in a dirty tavern, a man spilled his beer on her only nice dress. She was exhausted and angry, and even though she knew it would cost her the job, she lifted her hand to strike the man hard in the face. As she

was about to hit him, she quoted a line from one of the plays she'd memorized: 'Best beware my sting!'

"*The man grabbed her hand as it swung towards him and said in shock, 'My remedy is then, to pluck it out!' which happened to be the next line of dialogue in the play Mabel was quoting from! The two of them looked into each other's eyes, and in that moment, they went from hating each other to loving each other! That man turned out to be a great actor from a world-famous family, and soon Mabel married him and changed her name to . . .*"

And suddenly it dawned on Joseph who the story was really about.

"*. . . Eleanora Marvel.*"

"Joseph!" said Frankie as she stopped the tape again. "Do you realize what this is?"

"Yes, it's the history of my family! But why would Uncle Albert want to keep these stories secret from me?"

Joseph pressed play. There was the sound of something clinking on the tape, and laughter. The second voice, farther away, said, "*I didn't know that! I like that story,*" and then the first voice answered with "*Me, too!*" and then there was more laughter and another clinking sound, then more static.

Joseph turned the tape over and pressed play. Amid the same clinking and laughter, a new story began about a child named Billy Marvel, on an American whaling ship. The ship was called the *Kraken*. Joseph remembered that name from the painting near the door . . . which meant he knew the ship was doomed.

The story unfolded as the wheels of the cassette turned, and Joseph was entranced by this tale of a boy and his brother aboard a ship at sea. *"The boy had stowed away, secretly following his older brother onto the ship in Nantucket and hiding until they were far out to sea. Marcus was furious when he found his little brother on board . . ."*

"Marcus! That's my brother's name!" cried Frankie.

Joseph grabbed her arm, but the story kept coming and they didn't want to stop the tape again.

". . . so they had to find him a job on board the ship. Billy ended up peeling potatoes in the dark galley belowdeck. He longed to be with Marcus up among the sails and the rigging, but Marcus told him it was too dangerous. Then one night, to entertain themselves during a long voyage, the crew of the Kraken *put on a play called* The Angel and the Dragon.*"*

The other voice on the tape said, *"They did plays on board ships back then?"*

"Of course! The year was 1766, and there was a long history of sailors putting on plays while they were at sea.

Billy was forced to be the damsel in distress because girls were not allowed on ships at that time. He was put into a wig and a dress and a bonnet. It wasn't very comfortable, but he didn't care because it meant he got to be abovedeck, looking up at the stars, and the moon, in the open air, with his brother.

"He was tied to the mast. The evening wind rushed through the bonnet and the blonde wig fixed to his head. The play began and Billy yelled his lines so all the sailors sitting in the audience on deck could hear him. The crew whistled and shouted back. Then a handmade dragon approached, and the crowd screamed as the dragon opened wide its jaws to eat the damsel. Billy, in his costume, pointed to the rigging, high above the deck, and all eyes turned upwards. There, hanging by unseen ropes, was the angel, played by Marcus, wearing white wings and carrying a sword and a lantern . . ."

Joseph stopped the tape, hardly able to speak. "That sounds just like the angel Leo drew, the one on the ceiling of the theatre!"

"This is incredible," said Frankie.

The story continued. *". . . He descended from above to a great cheer, but no one had noticed the huge dark clouds that had rolled in from every direction, and at that moment, a lightning storm struck. The ship rocked and*

Marcus became tangled in the rigging. It was up to Billy to help him, but Marcus fell and landed far below on the deck. Meanwhile, the crew tried in vain to save the ship, but the rain poured down and a bolt of lightning split the Kraken *in two, sinking it . . ."*

Even though Joseph knew this part was coming, he still felt the terror of the wreck.

". . . The only survivors were Billy, his brother, and the boy's beloved dog, Tar, named for the black patch around his eye. The three of them washed up on a strange little island, and Billy took off his soaking-wet costume, using the dress to make a pillow for his brother. But Marcus's injuries from the fall were bad, and he died that day on the beach . . ."

Frankie stopped the machine. "Oh, Joseph . . . no! He died, too! Billy's brother Marcus died, too." She wiped her eyes.

Joseph put his hand on Frankie's arm again. "I know . . . I know. It's so strange."

"Okay. Sorry," she said. "Let's keep listening." She pressed play.

". . . and the dog howled with grief and lay by the angel's side, licking his face, until Billy was able to bury his brother. Oh, that beautiful dog. He was a good dog and true." Then the second voice, the one Joseph didn't

recognize, said, *"The door knocker! The dog!"*

Albert laughed on the cassette and, in his youthful voice, said, *"That's Billy's dog. That's Tar!"*

"I thought you hated dogs, Al."

Joseph couldn't imagine anyone calling his uncle "Al," but Albert Nightingale laughed again. *"He wasn't just any dog. It was Tar who first brought Billy to the theatre."*

"What do you mean?"

"They'd just arrived in London after being rescued from the burning island . . ."

"Wait! The island burned?"

Albert then told the story of Billy's rescue, how a fire he had started at his brother's grave spread from branch to branch until the entire island had gone up in flames, and just when he thought all was lost and he prepared to either burn to death or drown, a passing ship from England appeared in the distance, spotted the orange glow from the burning island, and came to save Billy and Tar.

"Their story was all over the newspapers," continued Albert, *"and Billy, with no other family back in America, decided to stay in England. He eventually found himself inside the Royal Theatre as it was being built. An artist who had been commissioned to paint a mural at the*

theatre listened to Billy tell the story of the shipwreck. He was so moved by Billy's bravery, and the loss of his brother, that he climbed up the scaffolding to the dome of the theatre, where he had begun painting a cloudy sky."

There was a pause on the tape, and it sounded as if Albert's voice cracked. He inhaled sharply and continued the story. *"He added an angel, with a sword and a lantern, and Billy knew it was his brother, Marcus, who was now immortalized on the ceiling of the theatre . . ."*

Joseph looked at Frankie again, amazed by how much of the story he'd encountered already without knowing it. The words *"You either see it or you don't"* had seemed like a warning to him, but maybe they were actually an invitation.

"And since the men who built the early theatres were mostly sailors who had returned from the sea," continued the voice on the tape, *"Billy felt right at home."*

Joseph remembered how the backstage of the Royal Theatre, with its miles of ropes and rigging, made him think of a ship.

So many thoughts ran through Joseph's head that he stopped the tape. "I think I need to take notes."

"Good idea," said Frankie, who ran to her room and came back with paper and pencil. Joseph quickly jotted down everything he could remember, names and dates and places, and then he and Frankie listened to more tapes.

There was a story about a silver necklace with a bird medallion. Marcus had given it to his brother as a goodbye present while they stood on the dock in Nantucket, before Billy had stowed away. Joseph wondered if it was the same necklace his uncle wore, which would mean the medallion was now over *two hundred years old.*

Joseph and Frankie listened to Albert talk about Billy growing up in the theatre, and how, when he was a young man, he'd found a baby, mysteriously abandoned in a basket behind the theatre on Tar's grave, with a note that said, *"Please someone raise my baby to be a good man in a bad world."* Billy never found the mother, and never knew why the baby had been abandoned, but he was grateful for the rest of his life for the chance to raise the child. Billy named him after his lost brother, Marcus, and the child grew up in the theatre, eventually becoming a great actor.

From there the stories jumped around. People appeared and disappeared, narratives stopped and started. Joseph tried hard to piece all the generations together, and he drew arrows between people he thought were connected, husbands to wives, parents to children, grandparents to grandchildren.

The history took shape: Billy Marvel was the beginning of a long line of actors. His son, Marcus, married an actress named Catherine Vine, and they had a child named Alexander. Alexander's stories on the tapes were fascinating because he'd lived his life as a wicked, dangerous man. He'd spent time in jail and been accused of murder, yet he was such a brilliant actor that every time he appeared on stage, the audiences would go wild.

"He eventually found himself with an unwanted son and no wife. The child, named Oberon, after the faerie king Alexander had famously played, was raised primarily by the stagehands in the theatre," continued the voice on the tape. *"Young Oberon hated his father because Alexander was cruel to him. He'd either ignore him or force him onto the stage. Oberon vowed he'd never become an actor like his father, but the pull of the stage was too strong. It was like a magnetic field he couldn't resist, and deep down he knew he was a great actor, greater even than his own father. So he returned to the stage after meeting his wife in the tavern. He and Eleanora became the most famous actors in the world. They travelled the globe, but always came home to the family theatre, which was now owned by Alexander. They were most famous for*

their roles as the king and queen in The Winter's Tale, *and they named their son Leontes, or Leo for short."*

"Leo! Of course!" said Joseph out loud. "That's how he got his name! He's named after King Leontes!"

"Shhh!" said Frankie.

"Meanwhile, Alexander grew older and slowly went mad. He moved into an abandoned prop room beneath the stage. There he spent his days reliving his past triumphs, speaking lines from his great plays to no one at all. He was the theatre's version of Miss Havisham, from Great Expectations, *still wearing the disintegrating costume of the faerie king, the role that had catapulted him to glory in his youth.*

"But it turned out that young Leo was the first Marvel in generations not interested in acting. His parents tried to force him onto the stage, like Oberon's own father had tried to force him. *But unlike Oberon, Leo was a terrible actor. He loved to draw and grew obsessed with the angel on the ceiling of the theatre. He drew it over and over again. Poor Leo was so lonely and lost. He felt like he'd been born into the wrong family, and he didn't know what he was meant to do with his life."*

Joseph had felt a connection to Leo the first moment he'd seen his photograph, and now he wished he could have met Leo, to tell him he felt the same way. He wished they could have been friends, and somehow this idea comforted Joseph. Being a branch on the same family tree as Leo made sense to him, and this strange new history made Joseph suddenly feel more alive, more *real*, and not quite so lost.

Joseph flipped the tape, anxious to discover what became of Leo. Maybe his fate would give Joseph a clue to his *own* future.

"*. . . In his madness,*" continued the tape, "*Grandfather Alexander was kind to Leo, and Leo loved him very much, even though he knew the stories about how cruel he'd been as a younger man. One of Leo's favourite things to do was sneak beneath the stage to visit him. Grandfather Alexander was always overjoyed to have an audience. He behaved as if he was on stage in front of thousands. And sometimes when Leo visited him, Alexander had moments of lucidity, and he'd tell his grandson stories about their family history, about the shipwreck and fire, the abandoned baby, the beloved dog.*

"*Leo was inspired by the stories of his great-great-grandfather Billy stowing away aboard a ship four generations earlier. So he decided to run away, too.*"

Joseph leaned in closer to the speakers. "*Before the sun rose, Leo wrote a note to his parents, making it clear he didn't belong in the theatre. Then he set off to the docks to board a ship bound for India. While he waited for the ship, though, he saw a strange orange glow in the sky. Some intuition told him something was terribly wrong, and he ran all the way to his family's theatre. It turned out that earlier that evening, the doddering old Alexander must have knocked over a candle, or dropped a match, because the entire theatre was engulfed in flames . . ."*

There was so much fire! Joseph never imagined his attraction to fire could be genetic, something that reached back through the generations.

"Leo knew his grandfather must be trapped beneath the stage. And it was up to Leo to save him. He raced inside . . ."

Joseph's heart beat hard as he held his breath, listening.

". . . but the inferno was overwhelming. Beams came crashing to the ground, canvas backdrops and paper posters curled and dissolved in the heat, wooden sets and thick ropes helped carry the blaze from one end of the building to the other, as if the fire had a mind of its own. Everything was in flames.

"Through the smoke, Leo managed to find his grandfather, who was choking. Leo grabbed his hand and pulled him forwards, but just then, there was a terrible sound and something broke above him and . . ."

For a moment Albert's voice rose on the tape, then there was a click, and silence.

"What happened?" cried Joseph.

He hit play again, but the story had stopped. He played other tapes, desperate to find out. But there was nothing else about the fire in the theatre, or Leo, or whether he lived or died.

JOSEPH WAS OVERCOME by the story, and neither he nor Frankie noticed how much time had passed. They almost didn't hear the front door open.

Frankie looked at the clock on the bookshelf. "My mum's home early. Go and hide in my room!"

Joseph grabbed his notes, ran up the stairs, and slid under Frankie's bed.

An eternity seemed to pass in silence, but then Joseph heard footsteps.

"He's not in here," he heard Frankie say heroically.

"He's here somewhere" came Albert's voice from the other side of the door.

"Albert," said a softer voice, which must have been Frankie's mother. "Won't you tell me what's going on? Please let me help." She spoke carefully, with an intimacy that hinted she knew Albert well.

"It's fine, Barbara. I'm sorry to do this to you, to pull you away from the clinic. Just help me find my nephew. Then make sure I don't strangle him."

"That's not funny, Albert," said Barbara.

Albert must have approached the door, because

Frankie cried, "You can't go in my room! It's private. Mum, make him leave."

"Open the door, Frankie," she answered firmly.

"He's not in there, I swear."

"Frankie, move!" And with that, the door swung open and in came Albert. Joseph could see his shoes and the bottom edge of his long fur coat. Albert quickly found Joseph under the bed. He grabbed his arm and pulled him to his feet.

"Albert! Be careful," said Barbara.

"Get your suitcase," said Albert.

"No!"

"Joseph, stop it."

"I'm not going."

Albert ran his fingers through his hair. "*Please,* Joseph."

"Just tell me one thing," Joseph said. "Did Leo die?"

His uncle's green eyes, which had been as hard as jewels, suddenly went wide. He glanced quickly from Joseph to Barbara and back again. The oddest, saddest expression flickered across his face.

"Who is Leo?" asked Barbara.

"We heard the story about the fire in the theatre," said Joseph, ignoring her. "We heard *all* the stories."

"My tapes . . ." said Albert.

"It's my fault," said Frankie. "I made Joseph listen to them. Don't be angry with him."

"But we didn't find out what happened *after* the fire," said Joseph.

"Fire?" said Barbara. "What's going on? *What* fire?"

"Stop it, Joseph," Albert said. "Not here."

"Is there another box of tapes?" Joseph asked.

Albert's face had turned to stone, and he didn't answer.

"What happened to Leo? You have to tell me! Look at all these notes I took!" Joseph reached into his pocket and showed his uncle the papers. "Oh, Uncle Albert! I think I know the answer! If all the clothes in Leo's room are from when he was my age, and the only photo of him is when he's around twelve or thirteen, then he *did* die, didn't he? He never grew up!"

Poor Leo was like the young prince in *The Winter's Tale*, thought Joseph, or the Little Match Girl. Or Frankie's brother. He was the child who died for no good reason in the story. There would be no miracle for Leo. He was just *dead*.

Joseph's heart hammered against his chest. "And . . . his parents abandoned the house because they were so sad and . . . they moved to *America*! That's it! Isn't it?"

"Albert?" said Barbara. "Is anyone going to tell me

what's going on? Should I call Florent? Maybe he can help."

"Do you think I won't be able to handle it or something?" Joseph said. "I can handle it. I'm not a baby! And I'm not daft. I will work it out. Maybe Oberon and Eleanora had *another* child in America, a girl maybe, and she married into the Nightingale family, and that's how we're related. Is that it? Am I right? Tell me! Tell me!"

Albert was trembling.

"I'm going to call Florent," said Barbara.

"Then I'll find out for myself," said Joseph to his uncle.

"What?" whispered Albert.

"I'll find out what happened *myself.*"

Joseph was running out of the door before he'd even finished the sentence, and Frankie followed quickly after him.

IT HAD STARTED to rain. Joseph and Frankie were soaking wet by the time they got to the theatre.

Joseph dried off his glasses and pounded on the stage door. The old doorkeeper leapt up from his desk and poked his head out. He removed a cigarette from his lower lip. "Blast it! Scared me half to death." He wore a green jacket with a green tie and yellow shirt, which looked like it might have fit him nicely once, a long time ago. "Need to see the Queen, do you?"

"What? No! Sorry?"

The old man laughed. "I'm joking. Just knocking off for the night. What can I do for you?" He inhaled on his cigarette.

"We have some questions about the theatre. Can you help us?"

The old man exhaled a grey cloud of smoke and squinted. "Now? Tonight?"

"Yes, sir!"

"What kind of questions?"

"About the history of the theatre . . . and the actors who performed here. Do you know anything about that?"

"I should jolly well hope so! Been at this door for *thirty* years." He flicked his ashes into his palm and smiled. "Might know something. More than the Queen, anyway. Come back in a few days."

"It has to be now! Please!"

"Bloody hell. Come in, come in!" The old man held the cigarette in the corner of his mouth. The children followed him into his tiny office by the door. On shelves around the TV monitor were books of all sizes, and on the wall were signed photographs of actors. "My castle," the old man said. "Don't drip on my desk. Don't need a moat! Put your coats and hats over there. Good." He dumped the ashes from his palm into a heavy green glass ashtray piled high with the crumpled remnants of previous cigarettes. The air was hazy with smoke.

Frankie pointed to one of the pictures on the wall. "I've seen her on the telly."

"Oh, you can't imagine the people who've come through this door." The old man waved his cigarette towards the doorway to emphasize his point. "Every one of 'em knew my name and stopped for a moment to pay their respects when they came to perform. Sorry I don't have any towels. Are you doing a school report on the theatre?"

Joseph looked at Frankie, who said, "Yes! Exactly!"

"Strange time to be doing research," said the old man. "But you've come to the right person. Name's Penney. Unofficial historian of the Royal Theatre, so I can probably tell you just about anything you want to know, from 1821 till today. Just make it fast."

"What about before 1821?" Joseph asked.

"What do you mean?"

"What about . . ." Joseph reached into his pocket and pulled out his notes. They were rather soggy, but he flattened them out. ". . . when the theatre was built, in . . . 1766," said Joseph, reading from the notes.

"The theatre was built in 1821."

Joseph double-checked his papers. "No, it was built in 1766. I wrote it down."

The old man laughed. He placed his cigarette onto the ashtray for a moment. "Sorry, I forgot. It's *you* who's the expert, not me!"

"Well, I guess I wrote it down wrong. I mostly want to know about the Marvels, anyway."

"The what?"

"The Marvels. The famous acting family!"

"Do you mean the Kembles? The daughters played here many times." Penney returned his cigarette to his mouth.

"No, the Marvels! Oberon and Eleanora Marvel. His

father was Alexander . . . they were all actors here at the Royal Theatre!"

"Oh, wait. Maybe you mean Billy's family!"

"Yes," Joseph practically screamed with relief. "Yes! That's who I mean! Billy Marvel!"

"He was a sweet man. Always stopped to chat with me."

"You *knew* him?"

"Of course."

"But . . . that's impossible!"

"No, he worked here for a while. A talented young man."

Frankie and Joseph looked at each other, confused. "No. Uh . . . Billy Marvel must have died . . ."

"Yes, we were so sad when we lost him. We've been losing so many of our friends."

Joseph frantically flipped through his notes. "No, I mean . . . Billy Marvel died in . . . 1824!"

The old man inhaled on his cigarette. "Oh, dear. I'm not *that* old, son! Billy died, let me see. He died about four or five years ago, I think. One of the first, I'm afraid. Can it be that long already?"

Joseph's mind was spinning. Penney had to be crazy. He looked at Frankie with his eyes wide.

"What about the fire?" asked Frankie, as if a change

of subject might help get Penney back on track.

"Heavens! What fire?" asked the old man, startled.

"The huge fire that almost destroyed the entire building in 1900!" Joseph confirmed everything from his notes.

"Calm down, duck. Calm down! I think we just have a little mix-up on our hands, that's all. Now . . . let me think." Penney tapped his forehead. "I want to help. I really do. Could you mean the *Savoy* Theatre by any chance? That one burned down in 1864, and then it was bombed in 1940, and just last February it burned *again,* poor old thing . . ."

Joseph couldn't control himself. "No! I'm thinking of *this* theatre!" He had a feeling that the entire building could burn down around them right this second and still the old man would say he didn't smell any smoke.

"There was some water damage in 1928," said Penney, "and the original gold mosaic on the interior dome was replaced by the painting of the angel."

"1928?"

"The painting was done by an Italian artist, who finished it in the thirties," said Penney. "Came to England for the job. I'd have to look up the exact year. I do know it's considered his masterwork. Only work of his in England."

"No, no, no . . . That's not right! I have here in my notes . . . Billy and his brother, Marcus, were sailors on the *Kraken*, which sank in . . . *1766*. Marcus died and Billy came to the theatre after he was rescued. It was in all the papers at the time. The angel was painted that same year in memory of Billy's lost brother, Marcus! That must be when the Italian artist did the painting."

"But I'm afraid in 1766 there was no theatre here at all, only a cobblestoned street overrun with pigs and bales of hay. We weren't built for another fifty-five years!"

"Don't you see? You've got it all wrong. What you're saying can't be right."

"Well, that's the history," said Penney with a shrug as he stubbed out his cigarette in the glass ashtray.

"Then your *history* is wrong!"

"Facts are facts, I can't change them."

"But I know the stories!"

Penney shrugged. "I know lots of stories, too, but they aren't the same as facts, son."

Penney lit another cigarette. He inhaled extravagantly and exhaled through his nostrils. Joseph and Frankie put on their coats as quickly as they could and almost ran towards the door. Penney held it open for them, and as they stepped out, he said, "Listen. There used to be a man who came by the theatre all the time to see Billy

Marvel, the one who died in *this* century I mean. Maybe you can ask *him*. Quite a character, he was. American. He might know something . . ."

"You don't mean—"

"Named for a bird, if I remember correctly."

Frankie and Joseph turned to each other.

"Albert Nightingale?" said Joseph.

"Yes!" The old man pointed at Joseph. "Albert Nightingale. That's it exactly. You know him?"

Joseph had no idea at all how to answer that question.

JOSEPH FOUND ALBERT in the dining room, sitting by the window.

"Frankie and I went to the theatre. We talked with someone there named Penney about the Marvels. He said he'd never heard of them and I thought he was insane, but then he told us he *knew* someone named Billy Marvel! Someone he said *you* knew. I don't understand, Uncle Albert! It doesn't make any sense."

Albert's attention shifted momentarily to the right. Joseph turned, and there was Florent, his hat in his hands, standing on the other side of the fireplace.

"Hello, Joseph," he said. "I'm sorry you did not know I was here. I got a phone call from Frankie's mother, and I brought your uncle home."

"Oh," said Joseph, embarrassed, as he put his hands in his pockets and looked down.

"Your timing is good, actually," said Florent. "We were just having a little *tête-à-tête*. Although I'm afraid I've done most of the talking." He smiled. "Thank you, Albert, for offering the tea, and thank you for listening to me. I hope, perhaps, you will find what I said helpful.

Especially now." Florent gestured towards Joseph and tipped his hat.

Albert shut his eyes.

"Well, I must leave you two." Florent tightened the scarf around his neck. "*À bientôt*, my friends. And happy New Year to us all." Florent let himself out, closing the door behind him.

Joseph remained in the entrance to the dining room, staring at his uncle, whose eyes stayed closed.

Madge made her way down the stairs and slipped into the parlour. The invisible bird chirped and footsteps clicked across the ceiling.

Albert opened his eyes and looked at his nephew. He tried to sound calm but his voice quavered. "Joseph, you're soaking wet. Go and change."

"I'm not moving until you tell me about our family, and this house, and the theatre." Joseph's whole body shook as his uncle slowly stood and walked across the room. He hesitated for a long time in front of a small cabinet Joseph hadn't noticed before. His back was to Joseph, and his head was bent.

"Uncle Albert?"

Finally, Albert opened a door in the cabinet and pulled out a thick manila envelope. He reached inside and removed a large stack of papers, which he set on the table.

Joseph could see writing on the top page: *Aut Visum Aut Non.*

"Florent told me I should share this with you. Maybe he's right."

"What is it?"

Albert put his hand on the papers. "Go upstairs, change out of your wet clothes, and when you come back, I'll show you the rest."

"But what—"

"Go."

This time Joseph listened. He ran up to Leo's room, took off his wet clothes, and laid them out in front of the fire. That's when he remembered his suitcase was at Frankie's. He opened the wardrobe and saw all of Leo's clothing, hanging clean and dry. The velvet suits looked so warm and comfortable, and he decided to try one on. It fit perfectly. He put on some of Leo's thick wool socks and a pair of his leather boots. The small photograph of Leo was still in the pocket of his wet trousers, and he transferred it for safekeeping into the velvet trousers he was now wearing.

If Albert was surprised to see Joseph return to the dining room in Leo's clothing, he didn't show it. "Sit down," he said.

Joseph sat in front of the stack of papers.

"Go ahead, Joseph, turn the page."

Joseph lifted the top piece of paper and moved it aside. The next one read *1766*.

Albert nodded to him. "Turn the page."

Joseph wasn't sure what he was expecting . . . a typed biography, perhaps, or a family tree, but it was neither of those things. It was a detailed pencil drawing made of a million tiny lines that crossed and recrossed, forming the silhouette of a sailing ship as it floated on a dark ocean beneath a cloudy night sky and a white crescent moon.

"Turn the page," Albert said again.

The next piece of paper was another drawing, a close-up of the prow of the ship, which read *Kraken*. And next was a picture of a girl tied to a mast of the ship.

Joseph flipped through the drawings. The dragon appeared and threatened Billy, who was dressed as a girl; the angel with a sword and lantern descended from heaven. The next few pictures revealed this was all a performance on the ship, and then came the shipwreck, and the angel's death on the shore of the deserted island, and the gravestone that read *Here lies my brother Marcus, an angel*. And Tar licking Marcus's face on the beach, and Billy burying his brother, and the theatre in London, and the painting of the angel on the ceiling, and the generations that followed . . . Marcus and Alexander and Oberon and, finally, Leo . . . almost all the stories Joseph and Frankie had heard on the tapes. It felt as if he was looking at pictures of his own dreams, sprung to life.

As the pile of drawings grew smaller, Joseph prayed the story wouldn't end before he could finally find out what happened to Leo. He moved through the pictures faster and faster as he came to the burning theatre, and the flames, the terrible flames, that filled the paper completely.

"Turn the page," said Albert. But there was only a single sheet of paper at the bottom of the pile, and it was blank.

"That's it? Where's the rest of the story?" asked Joseph.

"That's where it ends."

"But there are *ninety years* between the fire and now! What happened during those ninety years? What happened to Leo? That's what I'm trying to figure out!"

Albert didn't answer.

"Did you draw these?"

"No."

"Who did?"

"Billy Marvel."

"What? Oh, you mean the one Penney mentioned. The Billy Marvel you knew as well."

Albert nodded.

"Was he related to us, too? Why didn't you mention him earlier?"

"Joseph. I'm so sorry. You're asking the wrong questions."

"What do you mean?"

"Aren't you curious *how* Billy knew these stories?"

"They were passed down to him through the family?"

"No."

"Then . . ." Joseph struggled to come up with the answer, but nothing he could think of brought together the lost threads of Leo's story in 1900, his uncle, the house, and the sudden appearance of the *second* Billy Marvel.

Then Joseph remembered the tapes.

"Was it Billy you were talking to on the tapes?"

Albert nodded.

"So, the stories were passed down to you by *your* parents? Or there's some other family historian who told you. Does my mother know all these stories?"

"No, Joseph."

"Are there letters around here somewhere? Diaries?"

Albert shook his head.

The back of Joseph's neck tingled. Something was wrong. A stream of images and thoughts swept across his mind . . . every teacup and urn and key and painting and chair and book he'd seen leapt towards him out of the darkness. Names and dates, curtains and earrings, ships and theatres and angels rushed by as if they were caught in a tidal wave. A great noise accompanied the pictures in his head, a loud, roaring wind, and above it all, Joseph said, "Okay, then, tell me! *How do you know the stories?*"

Albert gently put his hand on his nephew's shoulder. The world grew quiet.

"Joseph . . . *I made them up.*"

JOSEPH LAUGHED. "What are you talking about? No, you didn't!"

"Yes, I did. All of them." Albert was almost whispering. "I made everything up."

Joseph felt as if someone had hit him hard in the chest, and he was struggling to catch his breath and talk at the same time. "You couldn't have made them up! The portraits, the jewellery . . . everything is *real*! The person who drew these pictures is named Billy *Marvel*! You just told me that! And the angel in the theatre is real, even if the dates got mixed up . . ." Joseph waved his pages of notes towards Albert. "It's all proof! It's all real!"

"Yes, yes. The *objects* are real. And a lot of the names are real. Billy was real. But the *stories* are mine."

"I don't understand!" Joseph stood up from the dining table and started pacing.

"Come, Joseph, sit down and I'll tell you."

Joseph looked around the room at all the objects placed with such care and precision. He pointed towards the urn labelled with the plaque that read BELOVED.

"That's not Oberon Marvel in there?"

"Joseph . . . *that* was Billy."

"But who *was* he?"

"Read the inscription."

"It just says '*BELOVED.*'"

"That's right. My beloved."

Joseph could not understand what his uncle was talking about. "So . . . this is all . . . a lie?"

"No."

"No?"

"It's all a story."

Joseph's mind felt like it was going to explode. "You lied to me! You knew the stories weren't true and you let me think they were!"

"I never lied to you."

Suddenly Joseph remembered Leo, and he pulled out the photo from his pocket. His fingers shook as he opened the case and thrust it angrily towards Albert. "Who is *this*, then?"

"To me it's always been Leontes Marvel."

"But you're saying there *was* no Leontes Marvel!"

"There *is*. In the story."

"But the story isn't true! None of it matters!" Joseph's hand gripped the edges of the case. He couldn't bring himself to look at the photo. Joseph was afraid he might discover *he'd* never existed, either.

Albert took a breath. "Is that what you really think? That none of it matters?"

"Yes!"

"But what about your books, Joseph? I saw the collection you brought with you from school. Your suitcase was filled with stories. I saw Charles Dickens, and Roald Dahl, and Madeleine L'Engle. I know you love stories. Do you think *they* don't matter?"

Joseph thought of Penney at the theatre and he spat the old man's words back at his uncle: *"Stories aren't the same as facts!"*

Albert paused and said, "No, but they can *both* be true."

"No, they can't!" Joseph wiped the long streaks of tears from his cheeks, then ran upstairs and slammed the door.

"JOSEPH!" ALBERT CALLED. "Come back downstairs."

"Leave me alone!" Joseph felt as if he'd plummeted from a great height, as if he'd been standing on scaffolding that reached to the sky and the entire thing had crumbled beneath him. He could feel the bed, the blanket, the pillow, but he just continued to fall.

Footsteps approached, and soon the door opened and Albert came in. He sat on the edge of the velvet bed.

Joseph was lying on his stomach with his head buried in his arms.

Albert moved a little closer. He tapped Joseph on the shoulder, but Joseph wouldn't budge. A long time passed in silence.

"Joseph . . . remember what you said the first night you came here, when you told me you wanted to stay with me?" Albert asked. "Remember what you said about the window, and the house?"

"No."

"You do remember, Joseph. You said it was *beautiful.* I think, deep down, that's really why I let you stay. And that's why I think you'll understand what I'm about to tell you."

Joseph rubbed his eyes and turned his head. "Tell me what?"

"The story of the Marvels."

"I already know the story of the Marvels."

"No, you don't."

"ONCE UPON A TIME," began Albert, "there was a junk shop in the desert. That's where your mother and I grew up. That's the place you visited, Joseph, with the fireplace."

Joseph remembered his grandfather's house being cluttered, but he didn't know it was a junk shop.

"Nightingale Antiques, my dad called it. He was raising us by himself. I loved the shop. It was like a cave of treasures to me. Dad taught me how to restore everything, fix broken table legs, rewire old lamps, refinish furniture, whatever needed mending. When I was ten, I unearthed an old book of Shakespeare's plays from a box in the back. The cover of the book was a painting of a shipwreck, and it mesmerized me. I hardly understood the plays, but I loved saying the words out loud. I read the book again and again, along with every book about England I could find in the library. I started pretending Dad's shop was in London, and I'd make up elaborate stories, until every object in the place had a story attached to it. I discovered Dickens and read everything he wrote. I even tried to talk with an English accent, which I learned by watching old movies on TV. It used to drive my sister crazy, which is why I think it's so funny she ended up with an Englishman. You've really never heard any of this from her?"

"My mother doesn't like to talk about her childhood."

"I'm not surprised to hear that. Our mother left when I was just a baby, and Sylvia suddenly had more responsibilities than she ever wanted. She grew to hate everything about our lives in the desert, and she vowed to get away as soon as she could. She wanted money and comfort and ease, which she got with your father. Do you know how they met?"

"At university."

"Right. I idolized your mother, you know. She was so smart and independent. But when I was fourteen, she left for university, and by the time I was sixteen, she'd moved to London with your dad. She never graduated. I guess she didn't need a degree to be the wife of a millionaire. Well, I decided right then I'd move here, too, when I finished school. After all, I was the one who had fallen in love with the city *first*. By the time I got to London, though, your parents had already left for Hong Kong or Saudi Arabia with whatever bank it was your father had been given to run."

"So what did you do when you got here?"

"I'd amassed a huge collection of books about the city by that point, and one of my favourites was *A Child of the Jago*, about a terrible section of nineteenth-century London called Spitalfields. I basically showed up with a suitcase and the clothes on my back . . . sort of like *you* did, come to think of it, although I was a little older.

"Half the buildings in Spitalfields seemed to be boarded up and abandoned, but it was cheap, so I stayed. For the first year or so, I crashed on sofas and rented different flats in the area with the other immigrants who had come to the city with no money. I worked odd jobs at the market, at pubs, ran errands, whatever people needed me to do, and a few more years went by. Eventually I saved enough to buy my horse and carriage. I spent months fixing it up, and then I started giving tours around the city. Turned out I knew more about London than most Londoners. I made a good amount of money, especially around Halloween, when I'd give my 'Haunted Tower' tour around the Tower of London."

Joseph wondered why the words "Haunted Tower" seemed familiar to him. He wished he could have gone on one of those tours.

"At night, I saw shows as often as I could, especially Shakespeare. There's always Shakespeare playing somewhere in London. One night I dropped off Rachel with Florent at the stable, and I was heading to a pub when someone stole my wallet. I chased him into an abandoned building, where I cornered him. Turned out the hoodlum was just a kid, robbing me on a dare. He couldn't have been more than sixteen. He begged me not to tell his parents." Albert shrugged. "Anyway, that's how I met Marcus."

"Frankie's *brother*?"

"Yes."

"He *robbed* you? He was a *hoodlum*? Frankie said he was really nice!"

"Well, maybe to *her*. He was a tough kid, but I'd grown tougher living in Spitalfields. I took him by the arm and marched him to his parents. Barbara and Harry weren't divorced yet, and it wasn't a happy home. They had no idea what to do with Marcus. I almost felt bad for the kid. But my mind kept wandering to the abandoned building I'd chased him into. Even in the darkness, I knew it dated to the eighteenth century and it had incredible . . . *potential*." Albert looked around Joseph's bedroom.

"You mean it was . . ."

"Yes, it was *this* house. Well, I was just about to leave their flat when my eye fell on a lovely little wooden table in the corner. Barbara noticed me looking, and she told me Marcus had built it himself in school, two years earlier, before he'd started getting into trouble. He'd always loved woodworking. It was the only class he'd enjoyed.

"So I got a little idea and made a proposal to his parents. I tracked down the owner of the abandoned house, and once the papers were all signed and it was mine, I arranged for Marcus to help me renovate. He'd dropped out of secondary school, and manual labour would be his punishment, though I had a feeling it would do him good to get out of his parents' flat and *work*.

"We spent the first couple of weeks just emptying the house of rubbish. We eventually found the golden ship rotting on the floor of the attic. We then rebuilt the entire house from the ground up, with help from craftsmen in the neighbourhood: joiners, wood turners, ironmongers, upholsterers.

"Marcus and I tore out any modern additions that had been put in over the years, like electric lights and vinyl flooring. We tore down plasterboard and were happy to discover much of the original woodwork underneath. We pulled down walls and found old fireplaces that, with a little fixing up, still worked.

"I needed to replace some of the antique tiles that had been lost, and I was having trouble finding someone to help with that. Florent told me about a man he knew on the other side of town, a successful set designer who worked a lot at the Royal Theatre. In fact, I recognized his name because I'd seen so many shows at the Royal, and it was a pretty memorable name."

"Billy Marvel."

Albert nodded. "Billy had a most unusual hobby, it turned out. He collected antique tiles and, in his spare time, made new ones, using the original glazing techniques he'd taught himself. I went to his studio, where he was in the middle of designing the set for a play called *The Alchemist*. Plans and models covered every surface of the place. Down in his cellar, he had a clay-covered worktable and his own kiln, and aprons spattered with clay hung along the wall. He showed me how he painted intricate blue glaze onto trays of tiles as if it was still the eighteenth century. What could I do? I fell in love with him. I wish you could have met him."

Joseph thought of all the carefully folded clay-spattered clothes he'd seen boxed up in the attic and the mud-covered shoes in Albert's room.

"By then, I was living in the house full-time. I saw how focused and calm Marcus was when he worked on the house, so I offered to let him move in with me if he promised to go back to school, and if his parents agreed. To my delight, everyone quickly said yes. That's when

I found out Marcus was a sleepwalker. I used to hear noises in the middle of the night, and I'd find him in the attic with the ruins of the golden weather vane. I'd walk him gently back to his room and try to tuck him in as tightly as I could, like a mummy, thinking maybe it would keep him from getting up again—"

"Wait . . ." said Joseph. Tiny details of the drawings he'd seen earlier started to come back to him. "*The Sleepwalker,*" he said to Albert. "Did I see something in the background of the drawings, the words *The Sleepwalker?* Right? And *The Alchemist* and *The Haunted Tower.* Those names," said Joseph. "Each one . . ."

"Very good. They're all in the story. The names of some of the plays being performed. You've got a good eye."

Joseph rubbed his head and sat up a little more on the bed.

"So Billy moved in, too. He brought with him old furniture he'd collected from plays he'd designed, and he started to fill our cupboards and armoires with old costumes from the theatre. Stories had begun to form in my mind related to objects in the house, just like when I was a kid in my dad's shop. And Billy introduced me to theatre archives, where I'd spend long afternoons looking at old costumes and poring through programmes, books, and photographs. I began to dream of imaginary actors and plays, and as you noticed, I took the titles from our lives, too.

"Billy made dozens of new tiles for the fireplaces and sinks. They look like eighteenth-century designs, but the images are of people in the neighbourhood, our friends. There's one of Florent and the carriage. I'm sure you haven't noticed them. They're very hard to spot unless you're looking for them."

"I saw some when I was cleaning the fireplace in your room. I remember there was one of two men holding hands."

"That's me and Billy."

"You either see it or you don't," said Joseph.

"Exactly. Those were Billy's words. They became the house motto."

"I see it."

"I know, Joseph. You're the first one since Billy died. That's why I'm telling you this story."

Joseph didn't know what to say. "Thank you" didn't seem like enough, and what words were there, really, for a moment like this? He ran his hands across his velvet suit, as if he could touch the story somehow, as if he was wearing the story itself.

"Before we knew it," continued Albert, "Billy,

Marcus, and I had formed an odd little family in a house that looked like it had come from the past. One of our last big projects was the golden ship in the attic, which Marcus seemed to have already claimed when he was sleepwalking. It was finally time to fix it up and return it to its spot on the roof.

"I put Marcus in charge of that job, and he worked day and night on the ship. We tracked down a boatbuilder who agreed to come in and help. He taught Marcus how to reframe the ship, using actual techniques for building boats. They'd spend hours in the attic, removing and polishing the brass panels until they shone like new. Once it was finished, Marcus helped install it on the roof. And for the first time in decades, maybe centuries, the ship was free to turn in the wind. Strangely, once the ship was done, Marcus stopped sleepwalking. But he couldn't stop thinking about that ship, and the sea. We'd go mudlarking down by the river—"

"Mudlarking?"

"Collecting little things that wash in from the water, bits and pieces of London's history that have fallen into the river over the centuries . . ."

Joseph immediately thought of the treasures Frankie had been given by Marcus, and the things in the glass jars.

". . . We'd fill our pockets as we walked along the shore together, watching the ships go by, and talking about life, or the future, or whatever was on his mind. It seemed like ships had most captured his imagination, so for Christmas I gave him a book about their history and design. He pored over it every night.

"Then one afternoon, on his own, Marcus called the shipbuilder who'd helped with the weather vane and convinced him he needed an apprentice for the summer. He wanted to build his own boat, a real one. He was going to call it the *Kraken*. I think he'd seen the name in the book of ships I'd given him, I'm not sure. We felt so proud, like he was our own son. That June, after school had finished, Marcus borrowed an old car and headed down to Bristol, where the shipbuilder was . . ." Albert covered his face with his hands, then pulled a handkerchief from his pocket and wiped his eyes.

"What happened?"

"He never made it. About halfway there, a lorry made an illegal turn and hit his car."

Joseph closed his eyes for a moment to steady himself. He wanted to go back in time now, to make the lorry unswerve and miss Marcus's car. He wanted the power to make miracles happen.

"I owe so much to him," continued Albert as

he rubbed his thumb across the ship tattoo on his forearm. "I never would have found this house without him, and if I hadn't found the house, I wouldn't have met Billy." Albert wiped his eyes again. "But I also felt responsible, you know. It was because of his work with me in the house that he'd driven off that day. I was scared that Barbara and Harry blamed me, too. I didn't know what to do with myself. Then, one night, Billy and I were at the theatre and we looked up at the painting of the angel.

"Of course, we'd both seen that mural a million times before, but for some reason, that night, I thought to myself, *That's Marcus!* He may have started off as a hoodlum, but Marcus Bloom had become a kind of angel to us. Suddenly all the stories that had been swirling around in my head began to crystallize and come together. *That's* when the Marvels really began. Does that make sense, Joseph?"

"I think so."

"At night, after supper, I would tell the stories to Billy, stitching them together one after the other. The story of the Marvels started to fall into place. I began with a child named after Billy who was connected to Marcus the angel. The ship on the roof became the *Kraken*, named after the boat Marcus had dreamed of. And Billy stowed away and ended up tied to the mast . . ."

"Dressed as a girl."

"Yes. Do you know why I did that?"

Joseph shook his head.

"Because of Frankie."

"Really? What do you mean?"

"Did Frankie tell you what she did when she heard her brother died?"

"No."

"She might not even remember. She was only four or five. She found a pair of scissors, cut her hair, and started walking around with Marcus's blue cap, the one she still wears, an old umbrella that had also belonged to him, and the book I'd given him about ships. It was sweet and heartbreaking all at once to see her walking around like that, as if she was trying to *become* her brother."

"I thought she was a boy when I first met her."

"A lot of people do."

"So Frankie was a girl dressed as a boy, and you made Billy into a boy dressed as a girl?"

"Right. The reasons were different, but it gave me the idea, anyway. Like a reflection in a fun house mirror."

"I once played Lady Capulet in *Romeo and Juliet*. It was an all-boys school."

"Exactly. It's an old tradition. And then Billy told me that sailors helped to build and rig the theatres of London when they first went up in the eighteenth and nineteenth centuries. Did you know that?"

"It's on the tapes," said Joseph. "Because sailors weren't afraid of heights and they knew how to use ropes and tie knots?"

"Exactly. You were listening carefully. That's why words common in the theatre now, like 'crew,' 'deck,' and 'rigging,' all come from the sea. So it made perfect sense for a theatre family to start on board a ship. Shakespeare inspired the storm and the shipwreck and the abandoned baby, among other things. The dog-shaped door knocker on our door became Tar, and my childhood Shakespeare book, which I re-bound with old leather covers, became Mabel Hatch's, whose dreams of striking it rich just might have been inspired a little by your mother."

Joseph never knew his mother had dreamed of "striking it rich." Until today, he'd just assumed she'd always been rich. It was hard to imagine her as a poor girl like Mabel Hatch, but perhaps even his mother had felt like she was born into the wrong family.

"I framed the original cover of the book," said Albert, "the painting of the shipwreck I'd loved so much as a child, wrote the word *Kraken* on the frame, and hung it by the front door. Everything in our lives became the stories, which we recorded on those tapes. Billy would sketch his favourite parts with his pencils by the fire. I loved watching him draw. He also repainted the old pictures we bought at flea markets, adding red hair and capes and curtains, turning the people into Oberon and Eleanora. He found the little leather case with the photo of the boy, and coloured his hair red, and he drew the angel, and signed Leo's name. He gave it to me for my birthday."

"What about your tattoo?" asked Joseph, pointing to the ship on his uncle's forearm.

"Billy designed this for our anniversary, after we lost Marcus. We both got one."

"But . . . haven't you ever wanted to continue the story, to decide what *happens* to Leo?"

"I can't continue the story, Joseph."

"Why not?"

"Billy got sick. He ended up at the clinic where Marcus and Frankie's mother works, and after he died . . ."

"The story stopped?"

Albert closed his eyes. "*Time* stopped."

Joseph ran his finger over the crystal of his watch.

"Is that why the last piece of paper is blank?" he asked. "Because Billy never . . ."

Albert sighed. "It's that blank piece of paper that makes me the saddest of all."

They sat quietly for a few moments until a bell rang in the distance, and someone knocked on a door that wasn't there.

"What *are* those sounds?" asked Joseph. "I've been hearing them ever since I arrived."

"Come, I'll show you."

JOSEPH FOLLOWED HIS uncle downstairs to a hidden door at the end of the ground floor hallway. He was surprised to see a modern little office, complete with a computer and a telephone (he had never thought to ask where his uncle had called his school from). There was also a small filing cabinet in one corner and a coatrack with several long fur coats, scarves, and woollen hats in another.

Albert opened a panel near the coatrack to reveal a series of knobs. "I didn't actually tear out *all* the electricity." He turned a switch and the noises got louder. Bells and conversations and carriages and footsteps burst through the air.

"Speakers are hidden throughout the house. It's quite clever, actually. A friend of Billy's from the theatre, a sound designer, helped us install it. We spent days recording everything; it was great fun. Ah, hear that voice? It's Billy!"

Joseph recognized the voice from the tapes. And then there was the familiar twittering and squawking Joseph had come to know so well. "What about that *bird*?"

"Oh, that was Billy's. A noisy yellow canary that was eaten by a kestrel when we hung her cage outside one afternoon. It made the local paper. Luckily we'd already done the recordings."

Albert then brought Joseph to the back parlour with the Christmas tree and the old piano. He turned up the gas lamps on either side of the fireplace and said, "Light the fire."

Joseph's cheeks tingled with pleasure as he stacked the logs.

"Cross them over each other, so the fire can catch," instructed Albert. "And distribute the kindling more evenly. And not so much paper."

Joseph struck the match, and soon the fire was crackling. Albert lit his pipe as Joseph sat down next to him on the sofa.

"You don't mind, do you?"

Joseph had come to associate the smell of pipe tobacco with the house, and it mingled so deeply with the pine and fire and wood that he couldn't imagine the house smelling any other way. Albert's green eyes were flecked with gold from the firelight, and he unconsciously lifted the bird charm he wore around his neck, rubbing it between his finger and thumb.

"That's the necklace Leo wears, isn't it?" asked

Joseph. "The one his grandfather gave him that once belonged to Billy."

Albert nodded. "Billy, *my* Billy, gave it to me soon after we met. Said it was a nightingale, like me. We then put it into the story."

Joseph looked at the back window. It had grown dark outside, and the glass turned into a mirror. It reflected the room, creating a shadow world that was just out of reach, where Joseph could see another fireplace, and another fire.

"Uncle Albert?"

"Yes?"

"Frankie said you go to her mother's clinic."

Albert puffed on his pipe, but didn't look at Joseph.

"Are you going to die?"

Albert's eyes glistened. "Hopefully not for a long time, Joseph. Barbara is taking good care of me. I told her she has to keep me healthy, because even though time has stopped here, this house is still alive. But when I die, the house will die, too, and all the stories, and all the memories will disappear."

"No, they won't!"

"They will, Joseph. The house needs to be tended to, cooked for, cleaned, washed, scrubbed. It needs to be *loved*. It's not like a book you can just close and put back on a shelf."

"But I'll take care of it! I'll remember the stories!"

Albert reached over and tenderly took Joseph's hand in his. *"'Come away, O human child! To the waters and the wild, With a faery, hand in hand, For the world's more full of weeping than you can understand.'"*

"That's in Blink's book," said Joseph. "It's Yeats."

Albert gazed around the room for a moment. "A haunted house, an imaginary family, a crazy uncle . . . I bet this wasn't what you bargained for when you ran away from school, was it?"

"No," said Joseph. "It's better."

TIME COULDN'T BE STOPPED, not really. Joseph knew that, even though he was wearing a nineteenth-century velvet suit, had a broken watch on his wrist, and had just eaten a huge meal in an ancient kitchen. But the fire snapped in the parlour, and shadows danced, and the sounds of the past filled the air. Then, a million voices seemed to rise up outside the windows, and they said:

"Ten! Nine! Eight! Seven! Six! Five! Four! Three! Two! One!"

It was midnight, and Joseph had nearly forgotten it was New Year's Eve.

A great noise burst from the city as the clock in the hallway began to chime, and the entire world seemed to cheer at once. Fireworks exploded across the night sky, and glitter rained down over London.

The roar outside grew and crested like a wave until, within a few minutes, it finally dissolved against the shore and left behind a blissful quiet that washed over Joseph and his uncle.

"Happy New Year," said Albert quietly.

"Happy New Year."

The two of them sat together in the warmth of the cosy room, side by side on the sofa.

"Joseph?"

Joseph turned to his uncle.

"After the holidays, we'll make some phone calls."

"To who?"

"We'll try to track down Dr. Patel."

"Really?"

"No guarantees it'll help at all, but we'll try. Blink's out there *somewhere*, right?"

The fire crackled and the cat appeared from behind the piano on the other side of the room. She stretched her paws out in front of her, yawned, and silently jumped up onto the sofa. She settled into Albert's lap, and he gently stroked the back of her neck. "Good old Madge," he said. "My faithful friend."

"Why is she called Madge?" Joseph asked. "I don't think that was in the story."

"It's short for 'Her Majesty.' She was given to me by the Queen."

"Really? Is that true?"

"That's a hard question to answer around here, isn't it?" he said.

Joseph smiled. "Uncle Albert?"

"Yes?"

"Can I stay here? With you, I mean? You and Billy let Marcus move in. Even if St. Anthony's will have me back, which I doubt, I'd rather stay here."

"I don't think your mother would agree to that, and besides, you need to go to school. But don't worry. I have some ideas."

"You do?"

Albert ran his fingers through Madge's fur and closed his eyes. "I'm glad you came and found me, Joseph. I'd hate to think what I'd be doing right now without you. I hope you know that."

Joseph looked at his uncle in the flickering golden glow of the fire, and his heart nearly broke with love.

As expected, St. Anthony's expelled Joseph. But after a long series of phone calls, including one with Joseph's mother when she returned from her trip, Albert made arrangements for him to attend Billy's alma mater, a school he'd loved, with the wonderful name of Dragon's Head Academy. The new headmaster was an old schoolmate of Billy's, and Dragon's Head was within easy driving distance to London, so Joseph could visit Albert on holidays. The new term would begin in two weeks.

Once that was settled, Albert called St. Anthony's on Joseph's behalf, looking for Blink. But because Dr. Patel had left no forwarding address, there was nothing the school could do, and no one at any of the famous hospitals in London had any idea how to track down Dr. Patel without more information (and there were about a million Patels in the phone book). The road quickly came to a dead end.

Joseph told Frankie the entire story about her brother, the house, and the ship. She cried because she'd forgotten about the haircut she'd given herself, and

Marcus's umbrella, and his book of ships. When he was done with the story, he handed her an old envelope with her name written on it. Inside was a card that read:

You are invited to dinner
18 Folgate Street
Tonight at 7:30 p.m.

"What's this?"

"An invitation! Uncle Albert had me write them." Joseph reached into his jacket pocket, where he produced two more envelopes, one marked *Barbara Bloom* and the other marked *Harry Bloom.*

"My parents haven't been in the same room in years!"

"Uncle Albert's already arranged it, but he wanted me to deliver the formal invitations, because that's how you have a proper dinner party."

"I REMEMBER the kestrel, the one that ate your canary," said Harry Bloom after he'd handed Albert the dessert he'd brought from his bakery. "Birds don't make the local papers very often."

Frankie's father didn't say much else, but the others exchanged some awkward small talk about the weather and local Spitalfields gossip involving the market as Albert led everyone into the dining room. "Why don't we take our seats?"

The black table was set for five, and everything sparkled and shimmered in the candlelight. Albert put a record on the Victrola and took his place at the head of the table. Once everyone had settled in, he raised his glass and said, "I'm so glad you could make it tonight. Let's begin with a toast to Marcus, who brought us all together in the first place."

The adults raised their wineglasses, and Joseph and Frankie toasted with apple juice.

"To Marcus," they said, and his name seemed to illuminate the room.

"Thank you, Albert," said Frankie's mother.

"Everything looks wonderful."

Joseph helped serve the meal, and he made sure everyone's glasses remained full. Knives and forks clinked across the china plates, and the fire hissed in the fireplace. The invisible canary sang in the corner. Harry turned towards the empty cage, confused.

"It's a recording," said Joseph. "It's the voice of the canary you mentioned, the one that was eaten by the kestrel."

"I see," said Harry. "How interesting."

"Your house is even more extraordinary than I remembered," said Barbara.

"I couldn't have done any of it without Marcus. He . . ." Tears came to Albert's eyes, and Barbara put her hand on his arm.

"Albert, please. Tonight's about good memories, and being together." She gave a quick glance at Harry and then looked down, at the tattoo of the black ship beneath her finger. "This ship . . . Billy had one, too."

Albert nodded.

"Were they in honour of Marcus?"

"Of course," said Albert, drying his eyes.

"I never realized. That's beautiful," said Barbara.

"Well . . . yes. *He* was beautiful. But we felt so guilty—"

"Guilty about what? What are you talking about?"

"It's just, if Marcus hadn't . . ." Albert's voice caught in his throat. He took a breath and tried again. "If Marcus hadn't discovered his love for ships here, in our attic, he wouldn't have driven off that day, and Billy and I both . . ." Albert put his face in his hands. "I'm so sorry, I didn't mean to bring this up . . . it's just always in the back of my mind, the fact that I'm partially—"

"Albert, stop," said Barbara.

A voice rose up from the other end of the table. "Sorry . . . may I say something, please?"

Everyone turned to Frankie's father.

Harry smoothed down his hair across the top of his head. "A lot of time has gone by and many things have changed since that day. But, Albert, you didn't cause Marcus's death . . . it was an accident."

"Right, I know. But—"

"No, please. I've thought about this a lot. The truth is, you saved Marcus's life. We remember what Marcus was like before you showed up. He was heading down a bad path, he was angry and lost. Barbara and I, we didn't know what to do. I was not a very good father to him, I'm afraid. But you saw something else in him, you gave him a purpose, you put him to work and set him in the right direction. It's what we all need in life. A direction. I'm sorry I wasn't the one to see it. And I'm sorry he didn't have more time. I'm sorry Frankie didn't get to know him, but I should have said this to you a long time ago, Albert. I'll always be grateful to you and Billy for what you did."

"Me, too, Albert," said Barbara.

Albert tried to speak but no words came out.

"And by god," said Harry, his voice unexpectedly gaining strength as he gestured all around him. "Look what he helped you make! This house should be registered with the National Trust."

From outside, a dog barked, and everyone looked towards the windows. "Don't even think about getting up," said Barbara to Frankie.

"I'm not going anywhere," said Frankie, who gripped Joseph's hand beneath the table. She was wide-eyed, staring at both her parents on the other side of the table as if she couldn't believe this night was really happening.

Joseph served the huge *bûche de Noël* that Frankie's father had brought for dessert. And as they ate it, Harry, with some gentle prompting from Albert, talked about birds. He told everyone about the songs of canaries, the diet of kestrels, and the extraordinary migration patterns of nightingales.

The clock struck ten.

"What a delicious meal," said Barbara as she set

down her fork. "It was a beautiful night."

"You should thank Joseph," Albert said. "He did most of the cooking. And not only that, the whole evening was his idea."

"Is that true, Joseph?" asked Frankie.

He nodded shyly.

"Another protégé," said Barbara. "You must be proud, Albert."

Albert put his hand on Joseph's shoulder. "The house has a way of attracting the right people."

Joseph liked that idea, as if the *house* had brought him here.

The candles flickered and the fire roared. The dishes and crystal glasses that were spread across the table glimmered in the light, and morsels of unfinished food remained on the antique plates and serving trays. Joseph stood up to start clearing the dishes and his napkin fell to the floor. He felt a strange tingle run down his back as he stared at the napkin. *The dishes, the crystal, the candles, the food, the wine, the chairs . . .* he realized *this* was the dinner party he'd imagined the very first time he'd looked through his uncle's window.

That night, cold and alone, Joseph had thought he'd found a portal into the past.

But he'd been wrong. It was a vision of the future.

THE DAYS SLIPPED quickly by. The house became a hive of activity. Albert took Joseph shopping at the market and walked him through the long rows of stalls with Florent, introducing him to everyone. Albert began to invite more people over, and soon the house was full of visitors, day and night.

Joseph tagged along as his uncle led tours through the house, opening doors to surprise everyone with the candlelit wonders in each room, and leaving them alone, in silence, to find their own way back downstairs. People started asking about the Marvels, and Joseph loved refilling the teapots and putting out the half-eaten food for all the members of the invisible family, who he always said had just stepped out.

On Joseph's last day in London, he packed his suitcase and prepared to go off to his new school. He ran his hand along the heavy wooden post at the corner of the bed he'd been sleeping in for the last few weeks. The house, and everything in it, had come to seem as permanent as the city itself.

"Joseph?" called Albert. "Frankie's here to say

goodbye."

Joseph leapt down the stairs and met her in the dining room. She had her Polaroid camera around her neck and a book under her arm.

"My mum and I have been searching all over the flat for this." She laid the book on the table and opened it. It was Marcus's book of ships. "Look at this, Joseph. I can't believe I never saw it before! Look at all the notes Marcus wrote in the margins. And here . . ." Frankie pointed to some handwriting in the back of the book. "He wrote a poem." She read it out loud.

> *Standing on the roof at night, beside the*
> *golden ship*
> *I look across the city and I dream a wild trip.*
> *The waves are high, the wind is strong, the*
> *moon is white and full.*
> *I smell the salt upon the sea, a strong*
> *magnetic pull.*
> *I shout into the endless dark, awaiting the*
> *reply:*
> *"Away! Away!" It says: "Away! Now spread*
> *your wings and fly."*

A sound caused Frankie and Joseph to look up. Standing in the doorway was Albert. He smiled at the children, then vanished momentarily, returning with his long fur coat and his purple hat.

"What are you waiting for?" he said to Frankie and Joseph as they looked at him, confused. "Put on your coats and follow me."

Within half an hour, the three of them had arrived at a road that dead-ended along the river Thames. Albert pulled his fur coat tightly around himself, opened the latch on a gate, and walked down a long series of battered concrete steps to the rocky beach. He beckoned the two children to follow. Their footsteps crunched in the wet sand, and the water lapped against the shore.

"This is where I used to bring Marcus," said Albert. "This is where we loved to go mudlarking and watch the ships go by."

Frankie looked at the shore as if she might spot Marcus skipping stones into the Thames.

The children followed Albert along the shoreline, until he bent over to pick something up. He handed the object to Frankie, who turned it in her hand and passed it to Joseph.

It was a small, dirty white cylinder of clay. "Do you know what that is?" Albert asked.

Frankie shook her head.

"What does it look like?"

Joseph turned it in his fingers. "I don't know . . . it's a little like the pipe you smoke, I guess."

"Good. Yes. It's a piece of an ancient pipe."

"I once did a report on the Great Fire," said Joseph. "People threw all their belongings into the river to save them from the flames. Could this pipe be from 1666, from someone who was running from the fire maybe, and dropped his pipe, and it broke and rolled into the river?"

"Yes, it could." Albert motioned towards the shore. "I used to tell Marcus that all the history of London is right here. These aren't rocks and stones beneath your feet, you know. They're what is left of the city over thousands of years." Albert scooped up a handful of things from the beach. "Right here, see? This is a piece of a Roman road. Think of all the lovers who may have walked along this road. And this bit of brick? Perhaps it's from a house that sheltered a murderer once. And this shard from a teacup, which looks so much like the one you broke the other day? Maybe this one was owned by a king or a queen who sipped from it on their wedding night, or maybe it broke on the night of the Great Fire. Who knows? But I'll guarantee you this, every fragment you see here, every scrap, once had a story."

Albert casually tossed everything back into the water. "Walking along the shore here is walking on history," he said. "It's like walking on an endless catalogue of lost stories. But there are other stories waiting to be told, and they will be lost one day, too. Whatever the case, it's all beneath your feet, right now."

But I, being poor, have only my dreams, thought Joseph, remembering the Yeats poem. *I have spread my dreams under your feet; Tread softly because you tread on my dreams.*

The light bounced off the water and shimmered against the buildings on the other side of the river. Joseph walked, listening to the sound of what was beneath his feet, and soon he noticed he was alone. He turned and saw that Frankie had stopped beside Albert, and the two of them were picking up more treasures scattered across the beach. Joseph watched from afar as Frankie talked with Albert and filled her jacket pockets. Looking at the two of them, Joseph wondered for a moment if *Leo* had ever come down here to go mudlarking, his red hair shining in the sun. The vision seemed so vivid, but then Joseph remembered Leo wasn't real, and the boy dissolved like smoke into the winter sky.

WHEN THE CAR finally arrived for Joseph later that day, Frankie snapped a Polaroid of him and Albert standing together in front of the house. She then handed the camera to Joseph. "Take a picture of me!" She gave Joseph both pictures to keep, and took another one of him for herself. "Write me letters. You'll come and visit in the spring. I'm sure I'll have the dog by then! And we'll go mudlarking again and you can tell me when it's 11:16."

Joseph smiled.

She gave him a quick hug, then ran off without looking back.

Albert and Joseph held each other for a long time. Before Joseph climbed into the black car, which had already picked up his suitcases from St. Anthony's, Albert handed him a package. Joseph unwrapped it and found the small leather case with the picture of Leo and the drawing of the angel inside.

"Take good care of him," whispered Albert. "And I'll keep my eye out for someone named Blink. Or George."

"MASTER JERVIS?" said a sudden, jarring voice from the classroom door.

Joseph looked up from his desk, along with everyone else.

The young headmaster of the school stood in the doorway with a strange expression on his face. "I apologize for the interruption, Professor Milne. Master Jervis, will you please come down to the office with me?" He turned to the teacher and said, "Carry on."

"Come back quickly, Jervis," said the professor. "I'll hold the test for you."

"Back to your work, boys," said the headmaster.

Joseph gave his paper to the teacher and followed the headmaster into the hall, where he put his arm on Joseph's shoulder. Through the open windows, Joseph could see the trees outside bursting with dazzling green leaves. A warm breeze moved through the hallway.

"I didn't do anything wrong," said Joseph.

"Of course not, Joseph," said the headmaster.

The clicking of their heels echoed off the polished floors and bounced across the high timber ceiling.

"You've been a wonderful student. I'm so pleased you're here."

They walked down a wide wooden staircase to the end of a long hall hung with banners. The headmaster stopped at the heavy door to his office and pushed it open. The huge iron hinges creaked.

At first, Joseph thought the panelled office was empty, but then he saw someone standing by the gothic windows, on the other side of a massive desk. Sharp beams of sunlight streamed across the man's angular face. A hesitant gap-toothed smile appeared.

"Hello, Little Nightingale," said Florent. "I am here to get you."

Joseph looked quickly at the headmaster, who said, "We've already discussed it with your parents."

And Joseph realized what was going on. "It's Uncle Albert—"

"He's expecting you, yes. Come now, let's pack some of your things and we'll talk in the car."

He followed Joseph back to his dorm room. Joseph had a million questions he wanted to ask, but he couldn't bring himself to say the words that scared him the most, so he didn't say anything. While he filled his suitcase, Florent wandered slowly around the room. Joseph saw him pick up a book from his desk. The title was in fancy gold letters: *Vingt mille lieues sous les mers.*

"*Twenty Thousand Leagues Under the Sea,*" translated Florent. "By Jules Verne. This book I have not read in many years."

"We're reading it in French class," Joseph said. "It's hard to understand, but I found a line that Uncle Albert would love."

Florent opened to a dog-eared page where Joseph had underlined a sentence and written the translation in the margin. Florent read it out loud. "*'Let me tell you, Professor, that you will not regret the time spent on board. You are going to travel in a land of marvels.'*"

Florent and Joseph looked briefly at each other before Joseph went back to his suitcase.

"Maybe you should bring the book, to read to your uncle," added Florent. "It will make him very happy, I'm sure, and I'd love to hear you speak French."

"*D'accord,*" said Joseph in French. "*Mais ma français est terrible.* Worse than my Latin, I think."

"*Non!*" answered Florent. "*C'est fantastique!*"

"Can we speak English, please?"

"*Bien sûr.* Of course. Ah. Look." Florent motioned to the pictures by the bed, the ones of Joseph and Albert and Frankie and Leo and the angel. Joseph had cropped the Polaroids to fit in some frames he'd found.

"I think you should bring these with you, too."

"Why?"

Florent picked one up. "It's always nice to be reminded how lucky you are."

Joseph did not feel very lucky at that moment. "What do you mean?"

"Such a nice family you have," said Florent. "Keep them close to you."

Joseph slipped the book and the photographs into his suitcase, which he carried to the car. It was strange to see Florent driving a modern car and not the black carriage. Neither of them spoke for the entire ride, but the silence wasn't uncomfortable or awkward. By the time they pulled up to the front of Albert's house on Folgate Street, though, Joseph had begun to cry. Florent held him tightly and said, "I know, I know. Come with me, we'll go and sit for a minute by the old market and talk before seeing Albert."

Florent grabbed his silver thermos from the car and they walked to the market. To Joseph's shock, it was now a huge vacant space littered with rubbish and a few piles of leftover packing crates. Gone were the forklifts and crates of fruit and men in white aprons. Even the four-sided clock had vanished.

A couple of children ran through the cavernous

space, kicking a ball against the brick walls.

"What happened?" asked Joseph. "I heard Uncle Albert talking about the market, but I didn't know it was going to close."

The two of them sat on the ground against the far wall. "Ah well, yes. For many years, we fought to keep the market open. It was Albert who led the fight. But when Billy, well . . . you know, everything seemed to stop for your uncle when Billy died. Until you showed up, that is. But by then it was too late.

"They opened a new market in Leyton last month. Some of us followed, others just closed up shop and retired. We hear they are going to turn this old market into a shopping centre now. Who could have imagined *that* when we first moved here so long ago? Well. *C'est la vie*, no? Everything changes."

"What about you? What are you going to do?"

"Me? Ah, you know me . . . I always work. A little here, a little there. I still have my fish, but I've been helping your uncle more, too. And Barbara."

Florent scanned the empty market, then unscrewed the lid from his thermos, poured some coffee into it, and handed it to Joseph. It tasted horrible, bitter and hot, and Joseph drank it all. He'd never had coffee before, and he was sure that for the rest of his life the smell of coffee would remind him of sitting here in the ruins of the lost market.

Florent placed the lid on the thermos and patted Joseph's hand. "Another *tête-à-tête* for us, it seems."

Joseph nodded. "When Uncle Albert wrote to me, he always said he felt fine."

"He *was* doing well. We were lucky. And your holiday visit made him happy for the first time in years. He continued to lead the tours through the house for a while, and I think all the attention and conversation were very good for him. But a few weeks ago he took a turn for the worse. His health, I mean. The door stopped opening. Frankie's mother was taking care of him at the clinic, just like she took care of Billy. But he wanted to go home, and he wanted to see you."

"Why didn't anyone tell me sooner?"

"He wanted us to wait, until he knew more. He didn't want you to get the news in a letter or a phone call, and then everything happened so fast . . ."

"He's not going to get better?" Joseph knew the answer, but he couldn't help but ask.

"Oh, Joseph, you know . . . there isn't anything . . ." Florent squeezed Joseph's hand again, but he didn't finish the sentence.

They cried for a few moments before they stood

up and headed back to the house. When they arrived, Frankie came running straight up to Joseph and wrapped her arms around him. At the end of a silver lead with a leather grip held tightly in her hand was the white dog. He was barking and ran circles around them until they were all tangled in the chain.

"I'm so happy to see you," she said, wiping tears from her eyes. Her hair was cut, and she was wearing the blue cap. "My mum wanted Albert to tell you sooner, she really did, but you know Albert. He's so stubborn."

"It's alright," said Joseph, taking his glasses off so he could rub his eyes. "You got the dog. What's his name?"

"Her. Turns out she's a girl! Her name is Schooner."

"Like the boat? That's a good name."

Frankie untangled the dog from their legs. "I learned it from my brother's book. It's either that or Brigantine, which is a boat, too, and I could call her Brig. But I'm also thinking about Clipper, like the ship." Frankie wiped her eyes again. "Sorry. I should tell my mum you're here. I'm glad you're back."

Florent put his hand on Joseph's shoulder. "Are you ready?"

ALBERT WAS IN the dining room.

The black table, the chairs, the silverware, the goblets, the oyster shells and napkins as well as the birdcage and candles and almost everything else had been moved out. The room seemed as empty as the old market, except for a small wooden bed Florent and Frankie's father had brought downstairs. Albert was sleeping beneath a blanket, his face turned towards the portrait of Oberon, with Billy's urn still on the mantelpiece below it. Plastic tubes were connected to beeping machines next to Albert's bed. His face looked gaunt, his bearded cheeks hollow. His arm was draped across his chest above the blanket and the tattoo of the ship was visible. The bird necklace rose and fell with his shallow breathing.

Joseph got a chair from the parlour and sat beside him. Florent stood nearby, his hand on Joseph's back.

"Hello, Joseph. Welcome back," said Barbara quietly as she leaned into the room. "Why don't we just let him sleep for a little while longer, then we can wake him up and let him know you're here. Okay?"

Joseph nodded.

"Do you want something to eat, dear?" Barbara asked. "Frankie's in the kitchen with the dog and we're going to make something."

"No, thanks," said Joseph. "I'm not hungry."

Florent went downstairs with Barbara, leaving Joseph alone with Albert.

Joseph listened to Albert's laboured breathing and the occasional car that passed outside, and realized the noises were all wrong. He got up and went to the back office, where he opened the hidden panel and flicked the switch to ON. The sounds of the Marvels, their voices and footsteps, their silverware and bells and carriages, came to life all around him. Billy was alive again, whispering in the next room, and the ghostly bird sang once more.

Joseph returned to his uncle's bedside and, as if awakened by the Marvels, Albert opened his eyes and turned to Joseph.

"Uncle Albert! You're awake."

Albert raised his eyebrows. In a breathy voice, he whispered, *"You lived!"*

"I . . . I don't understand what you mean, Uncle Albert."

"Leo?" Albert Nightingale whispered. *"Isn't that you?"*

Joseph's heart beat against his rib cage like the invisible bird, and tears fell down his cheeks. "Yes," he said quietly. "It's me. It's Leo."

A smile spread across Albert's face, and he closed his eyes again.

Suddenly, there was a commotion from downstairs.

Frankie yelled, "No! Stop!"

Schooner, or Brigantine, or whatever the dog's name was, must have come free from her lead, because she bolted upstairs from the kitchen, barking wildly. She ran madly through the house. Frankie, Florent, and Barbara chased the dog, who had maybe spotted Madge and was panting and barking, her sharp nails clattering against the wooden floors and up and down the stairs. Joseph leaned over Albert. He remembered how much his uncle had hated that dog, and he prayed they'd catch her quickly. But she came bursting into the dining room, circled them frantically, and jumped, half-crazed, right onto Albert's bed.

Joseph was about to grab her but stopped himself. Florent, Frankie, and Barbara came barrelling in, but Joseph stopped them, too.

Everyone looked at the bed.

The dog had calmed down, as if she'd finally found the one place in the world she most wanted to be. She sat at the top of the bed on the crisp white sheets, gently licking Albert's face. A breeze moved through the house as sunlight burst in from above. Joseph watched as the dining room turned itself into a tropical island in the middle of an ocean.

The survivors of a shipwreck washed ashore. A dog, a boy, and an angel.

Joseph looked at Frankie, who took off her cap and held it tight against her chest.

He could tell she was thinking the same thing he was.

They finally knew the dog's name.

Joseph's voice travelled across the water.

"Oh, Uncle Albert! Look . . . Tar is here! Tar is here, too!"

Albert Nightingale
Keeper of a great secret on Folgate Street
The Spitalfields Times
Sunday 5 May 1991

Albert Nightingale, who has died aged 36, kept a secret world behind his closed doors on Folgate Street. Those lucky enough to enter it found a kind of "time travel device," built painstakingly over many years. The house was briefly reopened in recent months . . .

JOSEPH'S MOTHER FLEW in from Germany, and her driver brought Joseph to the hotel. They hugged, and she told Joseph about the flu that had kept his father from flying in for the funeral, and she complained about the luggage the airline had almost lost at Heathrow. As Sylvia Jervis unpacked, Joseph tried to tell her what had been going on in London, to fill her in on Frankie and her family, the Marvels and his time with Uncle Albert, but he wasn't sure if she was listening because she never seemed to stop moving. "I'm sorry, Joseph," she said finally. "The flight was terrible and I'm exhausted. I need to get some rest."

Joseph kissed her on the cheek and her car took him back to Frankie's flat, where he'd been staying in the study that had once been Marcus's bedroom. After a long night of difficult dreams he couldn't quite remember in the morning, Joseph and Frankie prepared for Albert's funeral, which they'd been planning together for days.

With Florent's help, they plunged the entire neighbourhood back in time. They spent much of the morning putting up hundreds of yards of black bunting from house to house, along the route to the church. They made sure black wreaths were hung from every window, doorway, and streetlamp. The streets slowly became a black river of people dressed in mourning as everyone poured outside to help. Members of a local secondary school marching band, wearing rented tuxedoes and vintage top hats, practised a piece of the Mozart requiem, and children were given bouquets of flowers to carry. At last, the music began and a procession formed. Albert's coffin, covered in a deep pile of white lilies, was carried in a nineteenth-century glass-enclosed hearse, rumoured to have come from the Queen's own stables. Rachel pulled the mysterious vehicle, her head down, as if she were in mourning, too. Straw had been laid across the cobblestones so the ride would be silent and smooth, and police stopped traffic.

Frankie and her parents walked right behind Joseph, who was wearing one of Leo's black velvet suits, even though he was quickly outgrowing it. He had tied the cravat himself. It was lopsided, but he didn't care. He also wore a pair of Albert's leather boots, and the bird medallion was now around his neck. Sylvia Jervis walked beside her son. When she tripped on the cobblestones in her high heels, Joseph caught her. He held her hand the rest of the way to the church.

The service passed in a blur of tears and music, and afterwards, people started filling Albert's house.

Frankie found Joseph standing alone in a corner of the hallway, lost in thought, and she said, "Come on, Joseph." She helped him take off his jacket, and she laid it over the back of a chair. He rolled up his sleeves and they got to work. Frankie stayed by Joseph's side, helping him hand out the gifts they had made from treasures they'd collected for the occasion while mudlarking. With black ribbons, they'd tied to each item a handwritten tag that read: *Albert Nightingale, 1955–1991. Aut Visum Aut Non.* On every tag they'd drawn a little silhouette of a ship just like Albert's tattoo.

A steady supply of food and drink surfaced from the kitchen, where Frankie's parents and a few others were helping out. There was so much to do and so many people to greet that Joseph was able to put his sadness out of his mind for minutes at a time.

Tar had been placed upstairs in a wire cage, and amazingly, she was sleeping soundly. Madge made herself scarce, although every now and then her golden eyes would flash from beneath a chair or behind a curtain, as if she were looking for Albert. A record was playing on the old Victrola. Frankie's father had supplied a nearly endless amount of cakes and rolls and sweets from his bakery.

Joseph's mother excused herself and spent most of the time standing outside the house, chain-smoking cigarettes in her black dress. Joseph knew she smoked more when she was nervous, and there was a growing pile of cigarette butts at her feet. He joined her outside for a while, standing silently next to her while she smoked. Her arms were crossed and her red hair was pulled back from her face beneath the wide black brim of her hat. He had liked holding her hand in the procession, but there was no way he could take her hand now.

The door creaked and Barbara leaned outside.

"There you are, Joseph. I was wondering where you'd gone to."

"Hi, Mrs. Bloom."

"How are you doing, Sylvia?" Barbara asked.

Joseph's mother discreetly blew smoke out the side of her mouth. "Fine, thank you, Barbara. Thank you again for taking care of Joseph while he's here. It's very generous of you."

"It's my pleasure. He fits right in. He's a sweet boy."

Joseph had never heard himself described that way.

"I'm sorry your husband couldn't come," said Barbara.

"He hasn't been feeling well lately. And besides, he

never actually met Albert."

"Really?" Barbara sounded surprised.

An awkward silence settled between them.

"You've lived in the neighbourhood for a long time?" asked Joseph's mother, changing the subject.

Barbara nodded. "Since I was a child."

Joseph's mother inhaled again on her cigarette.

Barbara glanced quickly into the house, then finally stepped completely outside, closing the door behind her. "Your brother and Billy were fantastic with our son, Marcus. I don't know what we would have done without them. And then, after Marcus . . . sorry . . . I'm not sure how much you know."

Sylvia took off her sunglasses. Her eyes were red. She put her hand on Joseph's shoulder. "Joseph filled me in a bit last night after I arrived. I'm sorry about your son."

"Thank you."

Joseph was glad to discover his mother had been listening.

"May I ask you something, Barbara?"

"Of course."

"Do you think it'll be long on the market? Will we have a hard time with it?"

"With what?"

"When we sell. Do you think the house is really

worth anything? The neighbourhood's a bit . . ." She didn't finish the sentence.

Joseph held his breath and gripped the bird medallion around his neck.

"Oh, Sylvia. Don't you think . . . excuse me for being frank. But maybe it's rather too soon to be talking about this?"

"I'm sorry, I didn't mean to be rude."

Joseph couldn't believe it. His parents were going to cause the destruction of the house as soon as they could.

"It's just . . ." Barbara paused, gesturing towards the house. "What he did here . . . it's sort of *special*, don't you think? You can see what the neighbourhood thought of him. And I know Joseph loves it here. When I think about all the work Albert and Billy and Marcus put into the house, and the story of the Marvels . . ."

"The what?"

"The family Albert and Billy started. I thought Joseph might have told you?"

"Oh, yes. He did. The family of actors."

"Well, finding out Marcus is a part of the story, it's as if a little bit of him is still . . ." Barbara wiped her eyes and took a deep breath. "I guess what I'm saying is, it's just too bad this all can't be . . . saved, somehow."

Joseph's mother turned to him and said, "Would you

mind getting me a glass of water, Joseph? My throat's a little dry."

He knew his mother just wanted to talk privately with Mrs. Bloom. So he went into the house and paused in the doorway to listen to the rest of the conversation from behind the door.

"I'm afraid my husband won't think we can save the house," he heard his mother say. "I'm sure he'll expect me to have an appraisal arranged before I leave."

"I thought Albert told me he was preparing a will," answered Barbara. "Do you know what *his* wishes were for the house after he . . ."

Joseph couldn't bear to hear any more. He ran up to Leo's room and threw himself down on the bed.

Eventually someone knocked on the door. "Joseph. Are you alright?" It was Frankie. She came in and sat on the bed next to him.

"My parents are going to sell the house." Joseph sat up, wiped his eyes behind his glasses, and leaned back against the headboard.

Frankie took a deep breath. "Let's not think about it today. Not now."

"It's the only thing I *can* think about."

Joseph and Frankie sat silently for a while. The clock downstairs chimed the hour. Out of habit, Joseph looked at his watch, and Frankie said, "Is it still 11:16?"

Joseph smiled and rubbed his fingertip across the glass. Madge tiptoed into the room, slinking around the door. She vanished and silently reappeared on the bed next to Joseph. She pushed against him with her paws, then laid her head on his lap the way she used to do with Albert. Joseph rubbed the back of her neck. The cat closed her eyes and purred.

"Do you promise to take care of Madge if the house gets sold while I'm at school?"

"Of course," said Frankie as she petted the cat's stomach. "But that's not going to happen. We'll stop them!"

"How?"

Madge darted off, disappearing as suddenly as she'd appeared.

"I don't know, but there's always *something* you can do, even if it's small. Like . . . when I decided I wanted Tar. I went out every day and I *looked* for her, even when it seemed like I was never going to actually catch her."

"My uncle once told me the house was alive," said Joseph. "He thought it was going to die when he died. He said he needed to tend it, and take care of it, and love it. I think he imagined everything was just going to *stop* the moment he died. Disappear. But he was wrong, wasn't he? We're still here. *We're* still alive. And so is the house! The house isn't going to die because *he* died. It's going to die because of my parents!" The hands of Joseph's watch glinted in the firelight. "I wish I really could stop time. It might be the only way to keep them from selling the house."

"No . . . time is *supposed* to move forwards," said Frankie.

"But what if you don't like what happens?"

"Then . . . you change it."

Night had arrived and most of the guests were gone. Joseph checked the dining room and ran his fingertips along the carved moulding on one of the glossy walls. He closed the curtains and soon realized he heard music. He didn't remember anyone putting on another record. He followed the sound to the back parlour, where his mother, lit by candlelight, was playing the Mozart piano sonata.

Joseph watched as she lifted her hands from the keys, covered her eyes, and wept.

The floor creaked beneath his feet.

"Oh, Joseph, you startled me," she said, looking up. She wiped her eyes with the backs of her hands and tried to smile. "You've never heard me play, have you?"

"No."

"Do *you* play?"

"I don't."

His mother smiled. "Sit down. Your uncle always liked this tune. I used to play it on the old piano in the back of the shop. Listen." She showed him the opening bars of the Mozart sonata, and the ivory keys felt satisfying and smooth as he tried it himself.

"Good, Joseph."

It was the first time he could remember being praised by his mother in a long time. He loved playing the familiar tune on the ancient piano. It came easily to him.

"Promise me you'll find a piano to play at Dragon's Head," said his mother. "It's nice to play again. I shouldn't have stopped."

"You can't sell Uncle Albert's house," Joseph said suddenly.

"Let's not talk about this now."

"When do you want to talk about it? We never talk about important things. This is important!"

"Do you want to bring it up with your father? What would you propose we do with it? Look around. It's a wreck."

"It's supposed to look like this! It's *beautiful*."

Sylvia sighed. "You know you're just like your uncle, don't you?"

"I am?"

"Yes. That's the problem."

"Problem?" asked Joseph, confused. "Is that why you sent me away when I was so young? Because I reminded you of him?"

"That's not what I meant, Joseph. We were *worried*

about you. I hope you realize your father and I have always wanted the best for you."

"You never asked me what *I* wanted, though. What *I* thought would be best."

"You were *six years old*! You needed guidance. You still do."

"But what if that guidance is . . ." Joseph paused.

"Is what?"

"What if it's wrong? Wrong for *me*."

Sylvia ran the back of her hand along Joseph's cheek, just the way Albert had done the night Joseph first arrived in Spitalfields. She then smoothed the front of her dress and stood up. "Where's the phone, Joseph? I need to call for my car."

Joseph brought her to the hidden office.

When she had finished, Sylvia said goodbye to everyone cleaning up in the kitchen downstairs. She and Joseph waited for the car outside beneath the warm glow from the gas lamp above the door. Sylvia adjusted her hat and lit another cigarette. It was halfway to ash when two harsh white headlights lit the night and the car pulled up and stopped beside them. The driver got out and opened the back door.

"You're angry with me, Joseph." The light above the door created a halo around his mother's head, like a picture in a church. "What do you want me to say? It's late, and I'm exhausted."

"I don't know. I just want . . . to *understand*."

"Understand what, exactly?"

"You, Uncle Albert, our family."

Sylvia made a little sound, almost like a laugh, and tossed her cigarette to the ground. "I don't think anyone ever really understands their family, Joseph. I certainly didn't." She turned away to wipe her eyes, and Joseph thought he heard her say something under her breath. He couldn't quite make out the words. It had almost sounded like *"a walk in amber,"* but of course that didn't make any sense.

"What?"

"We'll talk in Hamburg, Joseph. I'll be rested then, and so will you. We'll discuss everything just like you want . . . my childhood, your uncle, whatever you'd like. How's that?"

His mother stared into his eyes and paused for a moment. She stood completely still, as if she'd transformed into a statue. Joseph found himself thinking once again about the end of *The Winter's Tale* and the queen's return to life. He still felt angry that the young prince Mamillius hadn't been saved, too, and he thought about Marcus, but as he looked up at his mother's face, a new thought came to him. Maybe the play wasn't about miracles. No, maybe it was about the passage of time, and the need for patience, and the ability to forgive. Maybe Shakespeare was saying that even in a world where miracles can happen, there's still going to be pain, and loss, and regret. Because sometimes people die and you can't bring them back. That's what life is, Joseph realized, miracles and sadness, side by side.

At that moment, the statue shaped like Joseph's mother began to move, startling him out of his thoughts.

"Goodbye, Josie," she said. She hadn't called him that in years. "Be a good boy while you're with the Blooms, alright?"

Joseph's mother settled back into her seat until she was swallowed completely by the long black car, and the driver shut the door.

"READY TO GO?" Barbara asked as she stepped into the dining room, where Joseph was sitting with Frankie by the window. They had pulled aside the curtains and were watching a couple of mice scuttling in the shadows on the other side of the street. Frankie stood and went to get Tar's cage. When she returned, Joseph said, "I want to take a moment, if that's okay."

"By yourself?" asked Frankie.

"Just a little while."

"Okay, but don't be too long," said Barbara. "And double-check all the candles and fireplaces before you leave."

"Of course."

"Goodbye, Little Nightingale," said Florent, who had appeared from the hall. He was drying his hands after finishing the last of the dishes.

"Goodbye, Florent. See you tomorrow?"

"Yes! Rachel and I will take you and Frankie to the theatre, and we'll say hello to Marcus the angel!"

They all departed and, after a long and impossible day, Joseph finally found himself alone in the house.

He could already feel the place beginning to slip away from him. He turned up the sounds in the walls, stoked the embers in the dining room fireplace, and added another log. He went around the room lighting more candles and promised himself he'd take care of the house for as long as he could, even if tonight was the only night he had.

The dining room table, where the buffet had lain all morning, was scratched and scuffed. Joseph loosened his cravat, took out a cloth and polish from the pantry, and got on his knees. He leaned over the table at eye level, just like his uncle used to do, and he slowly, carefully polished the table until it shone like new. Looking out across the glistening black expanse was like looking across the dark ocean, and he could see his reflection in it.

When he got up to stretch, Joseph realized for the first time that day how tired he felt. Madge slipped in and curled up behind a chair as if she had no idea this might be the last night the house would exist as she'd known it. Joseph looked at the portrait of Oberon Marvel and the urn below it that read *BELOVED*. He retrieved a full set of plates and crystal goblets from the shelves and cabinets around the room and carefully set the table. He poured wine and gathered some food from the kitchen, which he bit into and arranged on the plates. He pulled the chairs away from the table. He set out the candlesticks and pitchers and goblets and silver trays. Finally, he placed a napkin on the floor beneath one of the chairs.

Joseph then took the drawings from their cabinet and gently set them on the table. One by one, he flipped through the pages.

All the details he'd memorized jumped out like flares in the night, names and titles and plays that now made perfect sense because of Albert. The story beneath the story made itself clear to Joseph, like an X-ray. Yet somehow the Marvels themselves were more real, more *alive*, than they'd ever been before. And by the time Joseph came to the end, he could feel the terrible heat pressing against Leo's skin, and he could hear the burning theatre as it cracked and fell around him.

He turned to the blank piece of paper at the bottom of the pile, the one that had made his uncle so sad, and Joseph realized *this* was the real gift Albert Nightingale had left him: the story. It was *his* story now, and he knew his own story was as unfinished as Leo's.

In *The Winter's Tale*, a character named Time announced to the audience that sixteen years had passed. If that were to happen, Joseph thought, Leo might find himself telling his children about how, when he was young, he'd rescued his grandfather from a burning theatre, and Frankie might send Joseph a postcard from somewhere exotic, and Blink might suddenly appear with a book in his now-steady hands, upstairs in Albert's house, which had miraculously survived into the future.

But Time didn't let Joseph skip ahead. The fire was raging around Leo *right now*, and the flames were going to continue burning until he did something about it.

So Joseph turned the page.

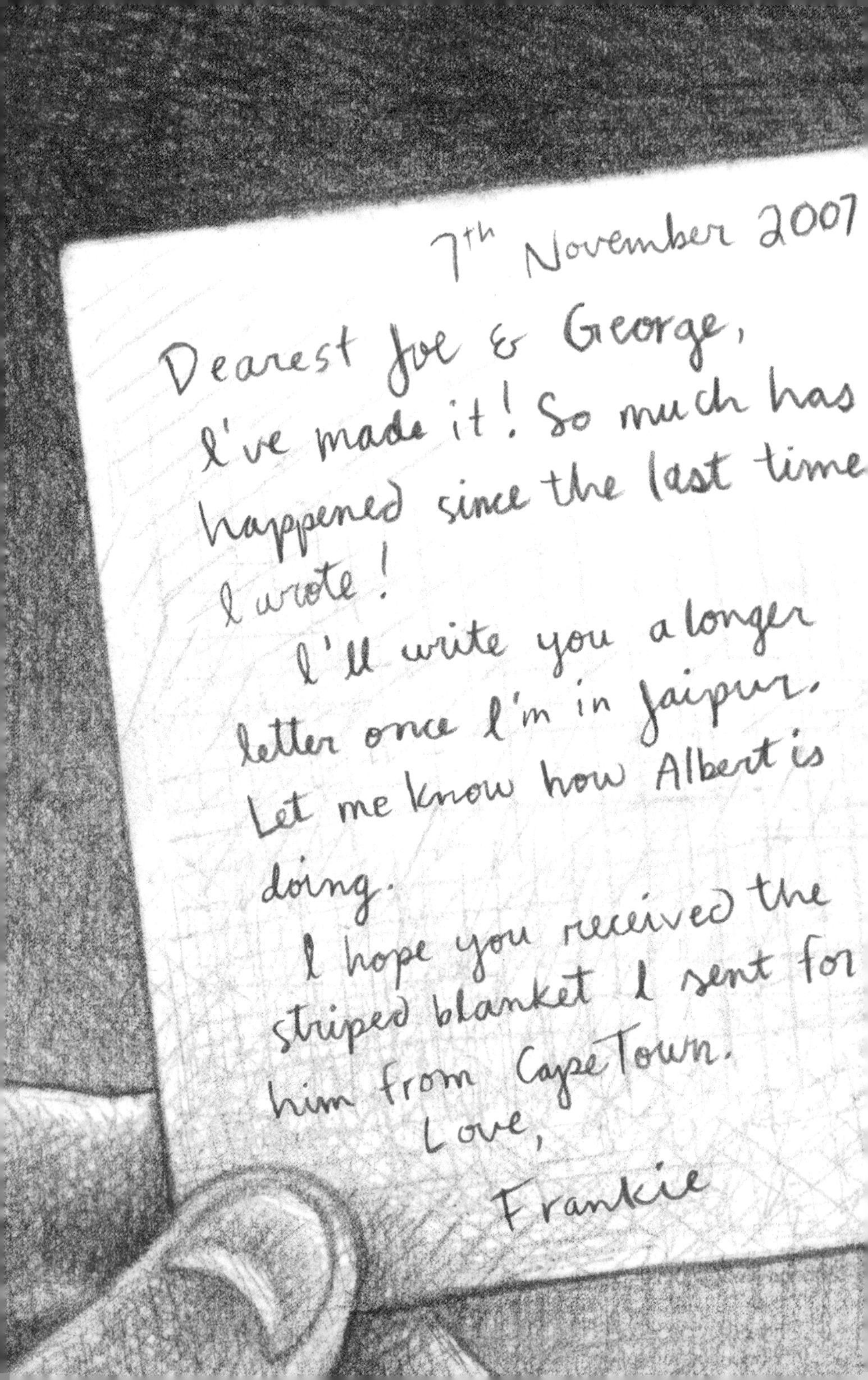

7th November 2007

Dearest Joe & George,

I've made it! So much has happened since the last time I wrote!

I'll write you a longer letter once I'm in Jaipur. Let me know how Albert is doing.

I hope you received the striped blanket I sent for him from Cape Town.

Love,

Frankie

The Nightingale House

18 Folgate Street

London

E1 6BX

UK

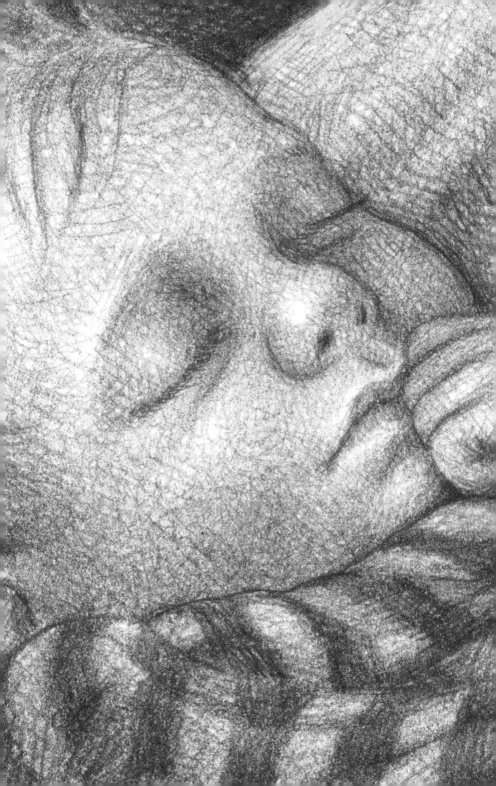

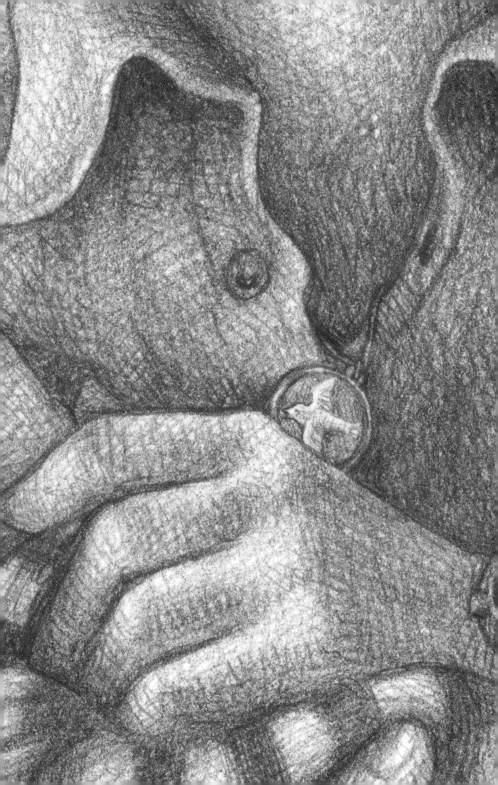

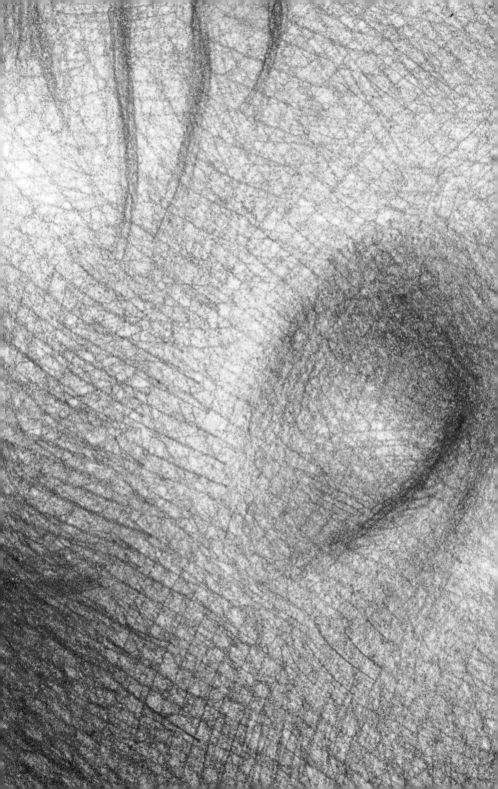

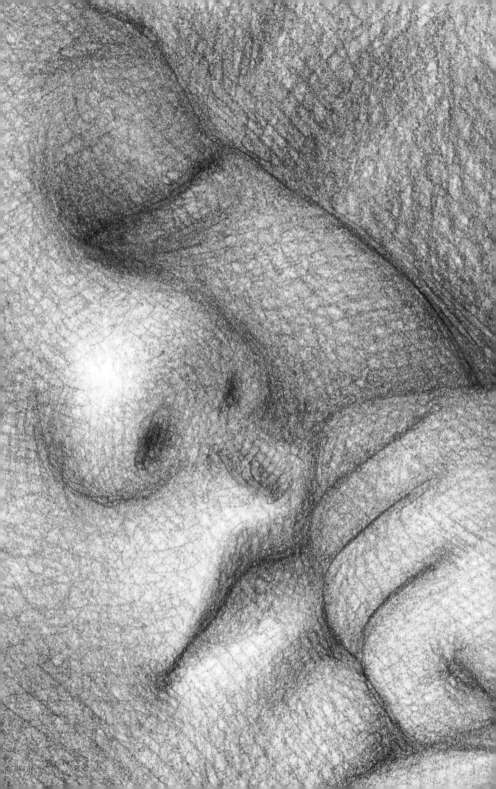

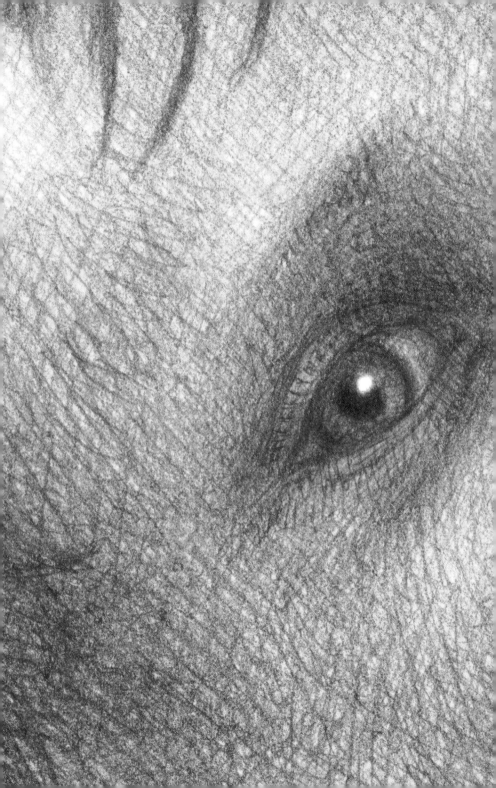

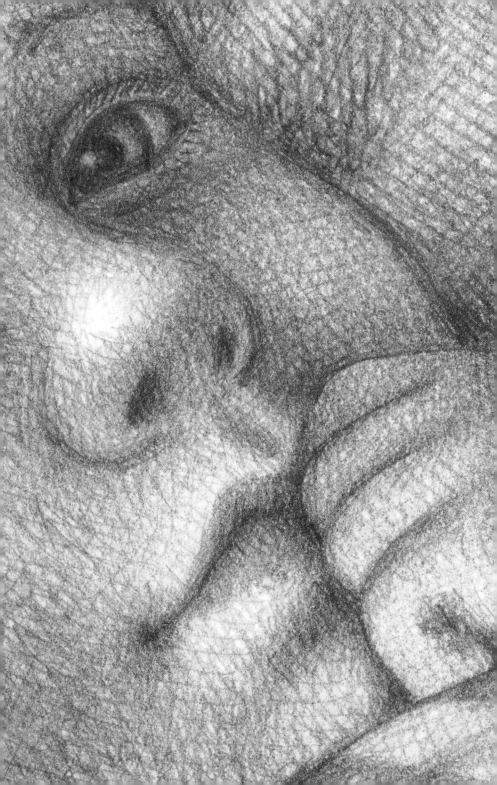

"Is this a true story?"
I said: "It is now."

    —*Wim Wenders,* The Act of Seeing

AFTERWORD

Much of this book is based loosely on the lives of two real people, Dennis Severs and David Milne. Dennis Severs created what is known today as Dennis Severs' House, at 18 Folgate Street, in London, England (www.dennissevershouse.co.uk). It is consistently voted among one of London's most popular and unforgettable tourist attractions.

Dennis died before I had the chance to meet him. But David Milne, Dennis's great friend and the current curator of Dennis Severs' House, has become a close friend of mine. He found his destiny one night in the 1980s when he stumbled upon a glowing window on a derelict street in Spitalfields that looked in on an eighteenth-century feast lit by candles. It is through David Milne that I feel as though I've gotten to know Dennis. He's generously shared his own life, as well as Dennis's, with me, and it's with his kind permission that I've borrowed so many of his memories for the creation of this book. In real life, Dennis created a fictional family to inhabit his mysterious home. He named his family the Jervises, which is the name I gave to Joseph, so in effect,

Dennis's fictional family became the real family within the structure of my story.

To make matters more confusing, the real lives of Dennis Severs and David Milne overlap in many places with the story of Albert Nightingale and Joseph Jervis. But they also diverge in many more places. *The Marvels* should in no way be seen as Dennis's and David's biographies. My story is a fiction built on the truth of their lives in much the same way that the story-within-the-story of *The Marvels* is a fiction built on the truth of Albert's and Billy's lives. But I happily acknowledge that my story wouldn't exist without the foundational bedrock of Dennis and David. I won't go into detail here about which parts of the book come directly from Dennis or David, but I will share with you one story . . .

On a cold winter's night a few years back, David Milne invited me to Dennis Severs' House when it was closed to the public. He made a fire in the dining room, and for an hour or two we talked. That entire time, David polished the black dining room table, balancing on his knees, checking every inch of the surface of the table to make sure it was smooth and perfect. I'm sure David didn't give this a second thought. To him, he was just polishing the table. But I remember thinking it was one of the most beautiful things I'd ever witnessed.

That's what love and devotion look like, I thought as I watched him so lovingly caress that tabletop. I've never forgotten that moment, and I gave it to Joseph at the end of this book to show how much he loved his uncle and his house.

I want to thank the Spitalfields Historic Buildings Trust for making sure that Dennis Severs' House was saved and preserved after Dennis's death. The staff at the house dedicate their lives to keeping the place alive, and I thank them deeply for their work.

I'd like to thank the following organizations and individuals who helped me with my research: Kathleen Dickson at the British Film Institute on Stephen Street; Stefan Dickers and the staff at the Bishopsgate Institute; Jonathan Lloyd, who brought me to the Garrick Club to view its collection of theatrical paintings and ephemera; Emily Cartwright at the London Transport Museum; Simon Sladen and the staff at the Victoria and Albert Museum Theatre and Performance collection; and Orla O'Donnell and Amelia Walker at the Wellcome Trust Collection.

I was thrilled to be able to tour a few of the beautiful old theatres in London. Darren Tooley and Jerry Katzman arranged a tour for me with David Pearson and Steve Hughes at the magnificent Aldwych

Theatre, and through the legwork of Eden Eisman, Karen Butler, Don Taffner, James Williams, Kirk Godling, and Eleanora McAlister-Dilks, I was able to tour the gorgeous Shaftesbury Theatre with David Scarr and Rebecca Storey.

But my fictional theatre, the Royal, is most closely based upon the glorious Theatre Royal Haymarket. My friend Harry Lloyd, a brilliant young actor who has performed on this stage, took me up into the rigging many years ago and first told me that eighteenth-century sailors came to London to help rig and build these theatres, and this conversation led directly to Billy Marvel and the *Kraken*. I later had the privilege of meeting Albert Crook, the owner of the theatre. I've since become friends with his daughter Kara McCulloch, the development director, as well as Cath Penney, the official Royal Haymarket historian. We spent many hours in their incredible theatre, going through ancient papers (many of the Marvel family's letters and documents are based on real documents from the Haymarket), and scuttling happily behind the scenes and through narrow, dusty backstage halls. Mark Stradling, the theatre manager, was enormously helpful there as well.

While I made up the names of several of the plays

that the Marvels perform in, all the books, authors, and poems mentioned in my story are real. *A Child of the Jago*, the book that brought Albert to Spitalfields, was responsible for bringing David Milne there in real life. The author is Arthur Morrison, and it's still in print.

Mabel Hatch's birth story is modeled closely on the life of an actress whose obituary I once read but whose name I can't recall now. The rest of her story, though, is fictional.

For anyone interested in learning more about Spitalfields, please check out www.spitalfieldslife.com, a brilliant and endlessly fascinating blog, written by a mysterious soul known only as the Gentle Author. This blog was an invaluable resource for me as I tried to re-create the world of Spitalfields in the early 1990s and prior.

Like much of my description of the neighborhood, the clinic where Frankie's mother works is a real place. It's called the Mildmay clinic, and their slogan is "Transforming the lives of people living with HIV." For more information about them, please visit www.mildmay.org.

Thank you to Barbara Barrie, who told me about her experiences performing in Shakespeare's plays; Charles Busch, who shared with me his expertise on the life of nineteenth-century actress Sarah Bernhardt; Simon Callow, who told me stories and shared with me his books on Dickens and Shakespeare; Tom French, who made a million photocopies for me at Ryman in London while I was living there researching the book; Brad Schnell, who helped me scan the drawings and make several dummies; Nayan Shah, who told me about the Indian diaspora and the history of the Patel name; and the Spector family, who photographed toy theatres in an ancient museum in Barcelona for me. Thank you to Jordan Spector and to Kait Feldmann, who helped me with Leo's handwriting and Frankie's handwriting, respectively.

Thank you to the following people, who patiently listened to my ideas and looked at the drawings and offered their invaluable advice: Matthew Burgess; Simon Costin; Jennifer Hunt; Dan Hurlin; Paul Kieve; Elizabeth, Daniel, and Storey Littleton; Marion Lloyd; Abigail Lopez; Stuart Maunder; Martin Moran; Ida Pearle; Jenna Rossi-Camus; Pam Muñoz Ryan; and Sarah Weeks.

Thank you to Ben Stephenson for help with many of the American to British translations. And thank you to Miriam Farbey, Peter Matthews, Samantha Smith, and Helen Thomas at Scholastic UK for their insights as well.

Throughout the book, I've used British spelling and diction, since the story takes place entirely in London. Some characters, like Albert, who are American, use a mixture of American and British phrases (and Joseph has grown up around the world so he also has a slightly mixed-up way of speaking), but for the most part, I've tried to create a book that would feel authentic to both American and British audiences.

Thank you to everyone at Scholastic Press, especially David Saylor, Charles Kreloff, Kait Feldmann, and Emellia Zamani. And once again, this book wouldn't exist without the work of my editor, Tracy Mack.

Thank you to David Serlin, for everything.

And finally, what follows is the obituary of Dennis Severs, in its entirety, which ran in the *Guardian* on 10 January 2000. Thank you to Jamie Wilson at the *Guardian* and writer Gavin Stamp for permission to reproduce it. You may notice that I borrowed a few phrases from it for Albert Nightingale's obituary.

No piece of writing I've found captures the spirit of the real house as closely as this.

Dennis Severs
Creator of a three-dimensional historical novel,
written in brick and candlelight in Spitalfields
Gavin Stamp
The Guardian, *Monday 10 January 2000*

Dennis Severs, who has died aged 51, tried to bring the past alive in the dark and strange living house museum he created inside 18 Folgate Street, Spitalfields, on the edge of London's East End.

It became, as he described it, "a famous time-machine" in which those prepared to enter his empathetic historical imagination and to suspend disbelief (never mind mundane considerations of historical fact, conventional museum practice or conservation philosophy) could find themselves transported into a dream which illuminated the complicated and poignant social history of that ancient part of London.

Although sneered at by many who suffer from what he would have dismissed as "pigeonholed styles of intelligence" inhibiting creativity, Severs was a true original, an artist of perverse genius who created a three-dimensional historical novel out of bricks and mortar and timber and the objects he picked up for a song on countless stalls.

The social historian Raphael Samuel considered it "a magical mystery tour which dazzles the visitor with a succession of scenes more crowded with memorable incident than the mere facsimile of what passes in the museums as a period room."

Dennis was one of those Americans in England who seemed to have arrived from nowhere, to have no past, no roots and who, so irritatingly, could not be placed socially. I first encountered him in the late 60s as the exotic friend of a Cambridge friend; he was then running horse-drawn open carriage tours around Hyde Park and the West End ("See Something Different Graciously") and seemed, even for me then, a little too starry-eyed about the charm of Victorian England. But Dennis was not a blazer and Brooks Brothers stereotype American Anglophile; he was humorous, generous, passionate, altogether unpretentious and engagingly camp.

I now know that he was a Californian, the son of Earl and Helen Severs, then of Escondido, who already had four sons between them by different marriages. In an unpublished guide to his house entitled The Space Between, *Severs recalled that, as a dreamy and imaginative child, he was regarded at one of his several schools as somewhere between "exceptional" and "mentally retarded."*

Storytelling earned him the respect of his peers, while the mania to collect began early. "Down deep," he recalled, "I always believed that one day I would travel past picture frames and into the marinated glow of a warmer, more mellow and more romantic light. There was one such light in particular, one that I saw in the combination of old varnish and paint, and that appealed to me as my ideal. By the age of 11, it was identified as English."

Severs visited England in 1965 and moved to London two years later, after high school graduation. He abandoned plans to become a barrister in favour of carriage tours, but then his stable, near Gloucester Road, was demolished by a developer. He bought the brick George I terraced house, to which he devoted the rest of his life, in 1979.

It was the right time: the campaign to restore Hawksmoor's great church nearby had begun, while the Spitalfields Historic Buildings Trust was fighting to prevent the erosion of that run-down, but mysterious, inner suburb. The artists Gilbert and George had already moved into Fournier Street while, more significantly perhaps, another pioneering resident was the late Raphael Samuel, whose analysis of the contemporary phenomenon of "retrochic" in his book, Theatres of Memory, *celebrated that restorative sympathy for the artefacts of the past that so moved Dennis.*

As he put it, he did not want so much to "restore" the house with its panelled rooms, "but to bring it to life as my home. With a candle, a chamber pot and a bedroll, I began sleeping in each of the house's 10 rooms so that I might arouse my intuition in the quest for each room's soul.

"Then, having neared it, I worked inside out from there to create what turned out to be a collection of atmospheres: moods that harbour the light and the spirit of various ages in Time."

The Spitalfields inhabited by Dennis was that of the novelist Peter Ackroyd rather than that of the historian John Summerson. And to illuminate these atmospheres for his paying visitors, Severs invented a family called Jervis who had lived there over the centuries and whose members had apparently just left each of the rooms entered.

With that openness and lack of prejudice which is America at its best, he cleverly combined low and high tech: real guttering candles co-existed with concealed taped sound-effects in settings which he constantly refined. Nor was this frivolous or cynical: visitors who giggled or who were otherwise unable to enter into the spirit of the enterprise would be summarily ejected.

Nothing could be less New Labour than Severs's achievement; for him, emotionally understanding the past was vital and his vision was holistic and therapeutic, almost spiritual. He felt able to summon up past eras not through history books, but through empathy with objects and places, to tell a fictional, true story "aimed at those who want to make sense of the whole picture of being alive."

Shortly before he died two days after Christmas, ravaged by cancer, bravely borne, after long being HIV-positive, his house was bought by the Spitalfields Trust, but it is hard to see how his creation can be sustained.

"Sadly," Dennis wrote, "I have recently come to accept what I refused to accept for so long: that the house is only ephemeral. That no one can put a preservation order on atmosphere." Certainly not now Dennis Severs has gone to join the Jervises.

• *Dennis Severs, museum creator, born 16 November 1948; died 27 December 1999*

Everything written here is accurate and quite uncanny, except for the last two paragraphs. With hindsight we now know that Dennis himself was wrong in thinking his house would die along with him. The house is thriving today under the care and leadership of David Milne, the Spitalfields Historic Buildings Trust, and the brilliant, hardworking staff.

The Jervises are still there, waiting for you, just out of reach in the other room.

Visit them if you can.

This book is dedicated to
David Milne and David Serlin

and to the memory of
Dennis Severs

Copyright © 2015 by Brian Selznick

Photo on pages 666–667 courtesy of Roelof Bakker

All rights reserved. Published by Scholastic Press, an imprint of Scholastic Inc., *Publishers since 1920.* SCHOLASTIC, SCHOLASTIC PRESS, and associated logos are trademarks and/or registered trademarks of Scholastic Inc.

The publisher does not have any control over and does not assume any responsibility for author or third-party websites or their content.

No part of this publication may be reproduced, stored in a retrieval system, or transmitted in any form or by any means, electronic, mechanical, photocopying, recording, or otherwise, without written permission of the publisher. For information regarding permission, write to Scholastic Inc., Attention: Permissions Department, 557 Broadway, New York, NY 10012.

This book is a work of fiction. Names, characters, places, and incidents are either the product of the author's imagination or are used fictitiously, and any resemblance to actual persons, living or dead, business establishments, events, or locales is entirely coincidental.
Library of Congress Cataloging-in-Publication Data available

ISBN 978-0-545-44868-0

10 9 8 7 6 5 4 3 2 1   15 16 17 18 19

Printed in China 38
First edition, September 2015

This book was printed on 120 GSM Woodfree UPM uncoated paper and was thread-sewn in 16-page signatures by King Yip (Dongguan) Printing & Packaging Co., Ltd., China.

The text of this book was set in Bulmer.

This book was designed by Brian Selznick and Charles Kreloff.

Harris County Public Library
Houston, Texas